KATHA REGIONAL

F.I.C.T.I.O.N

A Southern Harvest

Edited by
GITHA HARIHARAN

KATHA
Rupa . Co

First published in 1993 by
KATHA
Building Centre, Sarai Kale Khan,
Nizamuddin East, New Delhi 110 013
Phone: 4628227, 4628254

© Katha 1993

Distributed by
RUPA & CO.
15, Bankim Chatterjee Street, Calcutta 700 070
94, South Malaka, Allahabad 211 001
P.G. Solanki Path, Lamington Road, Bombay 400 007
7/16 Ansari Road, Daryaganj, New Delhi 110 002

General Series Editor: Geeta Dharmarajan
Assistant Editors: Meera Warrier, Renuka Ramachandran
Design: Neeraj and Pallavi Sahai

Typeset in ITC Galliard 10/13 by R. Ajith Kumar at Katha
Made and printed in India at Printwell Graphics

ISBN 81-85586-11-X   (hardback)
ISBN 81-85586-10-1   (paperback)

CONTENTS

KANNADA

TELUGU

PREFACE

The contemporary Indian short story is enriched by a multiplicity of languages and streams of writing; it can also be elusive for the same reason. In spite of its pitfalls, translation then is an unavoidable exercise to gain access to this wealth of fiction. The constant need for translation of outstanding stories in the various Indian languages to make them available to a larger audience is the starting point of this volume.

The necessity for translation has long been recognised; but not with equal enthusiasm the obstacles encountered during the actual business of translation. This applies to translation from Indian languages into English as well as from one Indian language to another, though the problems the two types of translation face are somewhat different. What both types clearly share is the status of second-class citizen that is all too easily meted out to translators, who often, quite literally, translate as a labour of love.

A more specific problem faced by Indians translating their literatures into English: often the original story is not written in the 'standard' version of a regional language. Mogalli Ganesh's 'Battha' ('The Paddy Harvest'), Allam Rajaiah's 'Manishi Lopali Vidwamsam' ('The Desolation Within') and Swamy's 'Vana Rale' ('Rain') are among the stories in this volume which use rural idiom peculiar to a particular geographical area, sometimes community. Here we face the problem of several levels of translation. In such cases, attempts to render the idiomatic flavour of the original in a colloquial English equivalent could misfire. It often seems that the safer option is the lesser evil — conventional English which loses much of the linguistic nature and richness of the original, but which at least does not jar, with say the incongruous use of Black American English by peasants in Andhra.

On the other hand, it is impossible to remain satisfied with the kind of translation we generally have to make do with — the literal kind ranging from the obscure to the banal, intent on not losing any-thing of the original.

Beginning with the premise that a translation can never *be* the original, the challenge it faces is that it has to find or fashion an appropriate equivalent idiom in the language it is taking the original story to. Perhaps the starting point of a concerted effort at 'creative' translation is recalling and reasserting the inherited tradition in India — 'rupantar' or change of form. Translation then need not always be a process of reduction: despite the loss involved, it can also mean renewal.

A Southern Harvest is an attempt to apply this criterion of enjoyable, 'live' translations to short fiction in the Indian languages. The focus on the short story is a useful one. The short story's concentrated intensity, and its allowance for suggestiveness and a variety of styles and ap-proaches, enable it to function as a signpost of dominant styles, themes and streams of writing in a particular language.

In addition, the division of *A Southern Harvest* into four language sections allows each part to be introduced through a brief overview of the short story as it has developed in that particular language. The introductions — written by writers and critics of the four literatures — identify some of the predominant themes, styles and movements in the contemporary short fiction of the language. They place the selected stories in a wider, more complete context, so that the stories need not be read in isolation, but as some significant facets of a lively, growing form of literary endeavour.

A few words about the choice of stories in *A Southern Harvest:* the writers represented include both 'newcomers' as well as those with established reputations. All the stories, written over the last ten to fifteen years, have been translated into English for the first time in this volume.

No conscious attempt was made to select 'representative' stories on the basis of geographical area, rural/urban themes, gender or commu-nity. But in its attempt to identify some of the dominant streams of writing, the anthology inevitably brings together a variety of viewpoints and backgrounds, from 'urban feminist' to Muslim community to dalit villages. At the same time, in spite of not being selected on the basis of any premeditated themes, the stories seem to have arranged themselves in a strikingly discernible pattern. The images that recur are those of poverty, pauperisation, dispossession and powerlessness — all the ground-level realities we have to face today. But while we do not hear any harvest songs in these stories, the writers weave in, along with the rage and pathos, the compassion and humour in the lives of people 'waiting eternally, devoutly, for some joyous event.'

A volume like this is necessarily the result of teamwork, particularly since an editor with fluency in four Indian languages is rare. I would especially like to thank K. Ayyappa Paniker, Ashokamitran, D.R. Nagaraj and Kethu Viswanatha Reddy for writing the introductory notes; and for providing ideas, stories and criticism with unflagging interest and patience.

As the task of collecting and translating stories got under way, the anthology also acquired a special network of friends who helped with addresses, stories, and above all, their time. These include Paul Zacharia, Sujit Mukherjee, G.P. Deshpande, P.P.C. Joshi and Lakshmi Holmström.

Among those who shared information, and their knowledge of language and literature, are the following: U.R. Anantha Murthy, Nakulan, Vasireddy Naveen, Rani Sarma, Ramachandra Sharma, D.Subramanyam, N. Kalyan Raman, Geeta Dharmarajan, V.K. Madhavan Kutty, E. Nageswara Rao, Meera Warrier and Mohan Rao. Most important, I must thank both writers and translators in equal measure; or perhaps thank the latter twice, since without them the entire exercise would have been impossible.

Githa Hariharan

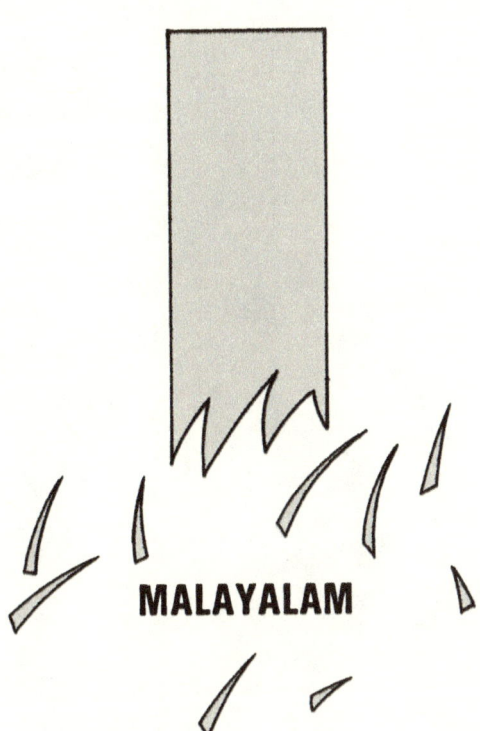

MALAYALAM

INTRODUCTION

The history of short fiction in Malayalam is more than a century old. During the past one hundred years there have been many ups and downs in the fortunes of the short story. The Malayalam short story made its appearance as a by-product of periodical literature about the end of the nineteenth century, but it came into its own during the 1940s. The forties and the fifties saw the short story as the most popular literary genre. The progressive literature movement discovered it as the most dominant form of expression. Karoor, Dev, Lalithambika, Saraswathi Amma, Pottekkatt, Varkey, Basheer and Kuttikrishnan were the acknowledged masters of the short story in Malayalam. They not only helped to focus the attention of the readers on the problems of the 'lower classes,' but also evolved a new literary language as close as possible to the spoken idiom of the common people. Not being scholars with advanced degrees in formal education, they used the limited space of the short story to reach out to the masses whose everyday life of depression and deprivation found a vibrant voice in their writings.

The fifties saw a remarkable change. The new short-story writers brought in a new sense of literary form and a new awareness of human experience. Literature became inward-oriented, more self-conscious in its choice of theme and style, and more preoccupied with the psychological concerns of individuals. It was like a transition from the 'puram' ('other-directed') school to the 'akam' ('inner-directed') school. T.Padmanabhan, M.T. Vasudevan Nair, O.V. Vijayan, Madhavikutty, M.Mukundan, N. Mohanan, N.P. Mohammed, Sethu and Kakkanadan belong to this generation of modernists. They did not write exactly like one another but the change in direction is most clearly marked in their stories.

The late seventies and eighties partly continued this strain, but the youngest generation of our short-story writers have already established

certain fresh ways of fiction-writing. C.V. Sreeraman, Zacharia, Anand,
Sara Joseph, Chandrika, Gracy, Ashita, Ashtamurthy and a few others
have slowly brought into being a new idiom and perspective. They do
maintain a grassroot-level contact with everyday reality, but there is
always a sub-text, partly transcending the mundane, partly even subvert-
ing it. For want of space only four stories could be included in this
anthology. There are yet others like U.K. Kumaran, Akbar Kakkathil,
Kochubava, Ramesan, Vaishakan and Joseph who have once again
brought the short story into the foreground. When quite a few of the
earlier short-story writers turned to the attractions of longer fiction, the
resulting gap was successfully filled by this new generation. Even the
popularity of the serial novel appearing in weeklies and monthlies in small
regulated doses is a homage the novel pays to the short story.

Zacharia was among the first to discover the fascination of the short
story with a sub-text. His use of fantasy, interwoven with what appears
on the surface to be a banal sequence of improbable incidents, showed
how even a mini-tale could carry an overtone or undertone bringing it
nearer the post-modernist poem. The semi-mock-serious tone he as-
sumes almost unwittingly helps him make oblique half-comments on
social reality. This is very clearly seen in 'Theevandikkolla' ('Rajan's Train
Robbery'). The revolutionaries and the party committee members are
there of course and Zacharia wants the reader to know they are very real
things; in the meanwhile the work of short-story writing too has to go
on. The robbery is not the story, because it misfires; the story is the
robbery, because it does not misfire. Every reader ought to take cogni-
zance of this.

Sreeraman, for all his personal commitment to party and ideology, is
his own master when he picks up his pen to write stories. 'Irrikyapindam[a]
('Obsequies for the Living') tells an apparently plain story of a family,
but the reality of the story is something created by the writer. The reader
is taken into confidence. The suggestive power or 'dhvani' of his
narrative prose comes from the mixing of many voices, some of them
ethereal and unheard. Making the unheard melody audible to the reader
is the secret of the post-modernist short story. Its essence lies between

the lines, as it were. The characters on the fringes, not the woman and her friend, but the priests for example, carry the implied reader's natural response to the story. Sreeraman is a true master of the narrative art.

When we turn to Anand, we see how he intones the whole narrative with a subtle, seemingly innocent vibration in his voice. The story includes, with disarming artlessness, the reader's possible comments on the story as well. The post-modernist feature of self-reflexivity is seen in several of Anand's recent stories. The form of the historical, even archaeological commentary he uses in stories such as 'Kayasthanmar' ('The Kayasthas') and 'Aaramathe Viral' ('The Sixth Finger'), gives a new dimension to the art of story-telling. Anand has the air of a researcher — he does not want his work to be approached merely as a story. This only underscores his unique inventiveness.

Manasy's story 'Devi Mahatmyam' ('The Goddesses of Arshab-harata') is a critique of the man-woman relationship, especially the husband-wife relationship in the Indian context, highlighting the para-dox and irony inherent in the situation. The traditional style of subju-gation through veneration — which virtually amounts to dehumanization — is presented in the story with bitter sarcasm. The writer undertakes not merely to narrate a poignant story; there is, in addition, the commentary on its signification. What the woman is deprived of in a patriarchal family system is subtly suggested. There are many narrative voices in the story — that of Veena whose child has been taken away from her, those of Lalaji's three wives, those of the narrator and her mother, and so on. That a woman should be patient like the earth is the lesson dinned into every female child. The writer makes the reader question this time-honoured conventional belief in the light of the self-awareness achieved by the female narrator.

The four stories in this volume may not represent all the divergent trends emerging in the contemporary Malayalam short story, but they do illustrate some of the most significant achievements in recent years. With the publication of an anthology of one hundred selected short stories covering a hundred years of their growth, the market for short fiction too has come alive. The continuity of the short story as a viable form of literary narration is thus assured. One looks forward to further growth in the immediate future.

Ayyappa Paniker

RAJAN'S TRAIN ROBBERY

ZACHARIA

At last Rajan decided to hold up and rob a train. In newspapers he had seen pictures of young revolutionaries holding up trains and shouting slogans while people of consequence, whose journeys had been held up, paced impatiently along the tracks.

'People of consequence,' Rajan said to himself, 'when I hold up your train, do forgive me. Think of me as a guinea pig that has somehow stumbled across the tracks. Consider me a mere object of study before you: I am someone forgotten by both revolution and government. I didn't have the skills to make capital of either. I shall not tire you with slogans. I shall only rob you, quickly, to quell the hunger of my little one, his mother and myself. Forgive me for bothering you.'

'Revolutionaries,' he continued to himself, 'forgive me for holding up the train alone; for accumulating capital without slogans. Before the boundless significance of slogans, my desires and the desires of my family are as insignificant as mustard seeds. Our tired voices are not even strong enough to cry out our helplessness. Forgive us this silent revolution of mustard seeds.'

Yielding to the grasp of a great sorrow, Rajan heard the lines of an old poem echo within like an ancient peal of thunder:

Does it matter whether the poor are born or die?
Forgive these vain words, O wise ones.

'My train, raising sparks along screaming rails, swaying passengers in their seats, embracing me within the majestic ripples of its heartbeats, knowing the wishes of my raised hands, shall come to a halt over the lily

fields. Then Appu shall hold the paper packet above his head and shout:
This is a bomb! Will his tired little voice rise above the impatient clamour
of the locomotive? I shall tell the driver: We do not want to hurl the
bomb. But if you move the train, this child will throw it. He is poor
and hungry. You must forgive him.'

'Then amid the sparkling sunlight and blowing winds of the fields,
below the flying clouds of the sky, as the pond lilies sway in laughter, I
shall crawl into the train like some insect. Begin my journey as a bandit
along its long vestibules and passages. The rusty old pocket-knife held
open in my hand shall make its way like a terrible stranger through
hushed whispers and frightened looks. But my friends, good people, this
is only me, your Rajan. This rusted knife is the sharp point of my hunger.
You must not be afraid. Neither this child nor I shall in fact harm you.'

'I shall only rob the rich. But couldn't there be rich revolutionaries
too? It does not matter; the wealth of the rich and the wealth of
revolutionaries look alike to the hungry.'

'I shall say: Forgive me for interrupting your journey. I am not angry
with you. You have money, I don't. My little child is hungry, he laughs
through his tears. I am not a thug or a bandit — just someone who is
hungry. May your children never cry with hunger. My son and his
mother are starving. I have no other way out. Here, here is so much
stolen money; you too can take some. I am not a bandit, merely Rajan
the impoverished one. When my little child plays, it is to forget hunger.
May your children never have to starve and play. May their childhood
be magical shady trees that keep them content. May divine grace shower
on them like the fruits, flowers and dead leaves of the shady tree.'

'But,' thought Rajan, 'what if the children in the train begin to cry
when they see my pocket-knife and my threatening stride?' He could
not bear to think of children with tear-filled eyes, crouching in fear. He
did not even like the thought of their hearing his tale of hunger and
need. He wished their brief encounter with him could be transformed
into a fairy tale in their eyes. Perhaps, for the little children alone, he
would make faces so they would laugh. But that would not suit a bandit.
He could still caress their cheeks though; perhaps give them a wink. He

could take them sweets if only he had some money. He finally decided
to take them bunches of flowers and all kinds of toys. These playthings
he would make himself, out of the tiny, unformed nuts of coconut trees
and the ribs of their leaves; he would weave balls with the leaves on their
fronds.

Rajan made a bomb with a green papaya that Appu had got from
somewhere, by wrapping it up in an old newspaper. He suppressed a
great desire to make a curry of it or to ripen it for eating. As if sensing
his desire, Appu said, 'Tomorrow I shall ask for another papaya — for
us to ripen and eat.' Rajan said nothing. Holding the papaya packet
above his head with both hands, Appu shouted with a wilted smile,
'This is a bomb; if the train moves I shall throw it.'

'You must not laugh,' said Rajan. 'The face of a bomb-thrower should
be full of cruelty. People should feel scared.'

Appu made a futile attempt to change his smile into a cruel look.

Then Rajan had to plan how he would stop the train. He had neither
the strength nor the knowledge he needed to rip the rails. Only organised
revolution could accomplish that. And even if he could, Rajan did not
want to do it; not even to roll a stone across the tracks. If the train
jumped the tracks and overturned, how many would bleed and die!
Could he end his hunger in their agony and death? He finally decided
to stand in the middle of the tracks, holding a red flag, screaming and
waving his hands like someone he had seen in the cinema. He knew a
spot where the tracks were a straight stretch, so that the driver would
see him from quite a distance.

Between the two crops, the pond lilies grew and flowered in the flat
stretches of fields. During the floods, the little raft made by Rajan the
child, a raft made of the shiny-white tubular piths of banana plants,
would wander over those fields like some kind of Noah's ark, carrying
lizards, spiders and other tiny creatures that had clambered onto it from
the flood waters. Along the spread of the muddy waters, beneath the
rain, beneath a sun that flickered, faded and shone by turns, and the
flashes of lightning that struck roots across the sky, the little lives that
had earlier bobbed and fluttered in desperation were now safe in the

silver lining of Rajan's raft.

Then summer would once again return with lilies. One summer, mounds of earth rose above the pond lilies, and over the pathways of Rajan's raft. Over the levelled earthwork the rail tracks began to stretch like a ladder fallen on the ground. One day a train decked with garlands, bunched banana-cuttings and buntings, like some giant dressed up as a clown, spewed great sighs as it passed along the tracks. Though it cut the world of his raft in two, Rajan loved the train. He loved its smouldering heart, its panting and wild clangour, its orchestrated rhythms. He loved the people too, who passed one way or the other before his eager eyes. By night, when the train broke into his sleep with its ringing hoots, it tunnelled paths of light through the thick darkness that hung below the flying clouds. It passed by like a gargantuan caterpillar, and Rajan flew along with it to the lands of his dreams that flowed with milk and honey.

When thousands of trains had passed by, and when thousands of revolutionaries and officials had rushed past to their sanctuaries of milk and honey, Rajan finally understood: I am only a witness to the passing of trains. My little raft, with its blessedness and grace, has rotted away by some arid shore of childhood. Rajan understood that hunger alone was his inheritance. 'Let my train also be imprisoned along the paths of my little raft,' Rajan thought. 'You long worms of light that flew by, humming through my nights, now let me halt and bind you to put an end to my hunger. When you lie waiting in my bonds in the fields of pond lilies, I shall walk through your entrails that swarm with my stale old dreams; I shall then draw limits to my hunger. You must let forth screams of delight; and bless the remainder of my little son's childhood.' Appu stood frozen with the wrapped papaya in his hands, and stared at a tear that rolled down his father's cheek.

In the morning, prepared with the wrapped papaya, the rusted pocket-knife, the bunches of flowers wrapped in a light towel, the toys of tiny nuts and leaf-ribs, and the balls woven from palm leaves, Rajan and Appu left home. Rajan said nothing to Lakshmi. He wanted to see her wonder and happiness when he returned with the money. 'We must walk fast,' Rajan said. 'We shall catch the eleven o'clock train in the middle of the fields.'

Only the most important item was missing. The red flag. Rajan thought he would take one of those flags in the party office, thrown aside after the elections in a corner of the verandah. When he reached the party office, there was some committee meeting going on. Leaving Appu outside, Rajan wove his way among the parked cars, quietly entered the building and picked up a little red flag from the corner of the verandah. From within the office he heard ⁺he languorous murmurs of the committee meeting. As he was leaving with the flag under one arm, he heard the question from behind: 'Who is taking the flag away?' His own heartbeat rang loud in Rajan's ears.

'It's only me,' Rajan said, holding out the flag. 'Just . . . thought I would tie it up over the house.'

'Come on. Leave the flag there.'

'Sir, aren't they just lying around? I am taking only one.'

'What do you think, is the flag public property? It is the property of the party. Not something you can just make off with. Drop the flag right there.'

Rajan wanted to scream. He wanted to tell the man that he *must* have the flag since he was going to rob the train by waving it, and that it was a question of his hunger. But he only pleaded, 'Sir, I shall return it.'

'Don't fold it or turn it around, hah! Hah! All this is accountable property I say! Accumulated by hard work at public collections. Put back the flag. Have things become so bad that anyone can take anything? Is there such a total lack of discipline?' Hearing his laughter, a couple of committee members came out into the verandah yawning.

'What is it?' they asked. Rajan, like some clockwork creature, walked up to the corner and put the flag down on the pile there. He then walked quickly past the gate and on to the road. Appu was near one of the parked cars, joyfully running his hands across its smooth, gleaming body. Rajan took his hand and said, 'Run! We don't have enough time to reach the big fields. The train will pass by. Run for the bend by the Whitewater

Stream!' And Rajan and Appu ran.

Panting across short-cuts, skipping down stone steps, crawling through parted barbed-wire fences, they reached the edge of a grass and scum-covered bog. Once across, they ran up the embankment through the flowering creepers. Their feet shattered the sun that lay burning in the bog waters between clumps of grass. Then the sherds of shattered light came together again across the bog waters and filmed over with the reddish ooze of marsh-weed roots.

Appu sat down exhausted among the creepers in full bloom, holding the papaya packet close to his chest. His drained, pale face was covered with sweat, but he was smiling. Making sure once again of the pocket-knife at his hip, the bunches of flowers wrapped in a towel in one hand, Rajan walked over to the middle of the tracks. The tracks which shone in the bright sunlight disappeared beyond a curve just ahead.

'But we don't have the flag, Acchan,' said Appu from the embankment.

'No. I am just going to wave my arms,' said Rajan, peering hard at the curve ahead. 'What will you do if I am run over by the train?'

'I'll run away crying,' laughed Appu.

'My dearest child,' thought Rajan, 'I cannot bear to think of you crying.' He then stood still, staring ahead at the tracks. He felt a cool breeze caress him.

'Keep your ears open for the whistle,' said Rajan to Appu. Appu replied, 'I can put my ear to the rail, Acchan. The rail will begin humming even when the train is still quite far away.'

'How do you know that?' asked Rajan.

'I put my ear to the rails once . . .' said Appu in his little voice.

'You need a spanking, Appu!' said Rajan.

And then the train came pounding past the bend. Rajan stood on the trembling wooden sleepers, threw both his arms high above his head and waved. The earth and the tracks shook as in a quake. Rajan wondered at the expressionless face of his train. 'Didn't even hear it come . . .' he heard Appu say from below. He waved his arms with all his might. 'Stop! Stop! Stop for my sake, stop for Appu's sake. Stop for the sake of the memory of my love. Be my child's prisoner for a minute. End our hunger . . .'

The shrieks of the locomotive and the rushing wind hit Rajan like a blow.

'Acchan, the train will hit you!' Appu shouted.

In a flash Rajan saw the face of his child among the bell-shaped flowers; a face crowded with desire, amazement and fear.

'My son!' Rajan leapt into the tangle of flowers. He rolled and tumbled down the muddy embankment, shattering the sun in the bog water once again. He lay in the water, red with the ooze of marsh-weed roots, like some substance under chemical analysis. Rajan lay back in the bog, his eyes closed against the flaring sun in the sky that seared them. He heard his train whistle, and fly across a sky drenched with sunlight; just as it used to through the nights of his childhood. When a shadow fell across his eyes, he opened them. Appu sat on his haunches beside Rajan, smiling down into his face. Drawing Appu close to him, Rajan said, 'That train whispered a secret to Acchan.'

'What was it, Acchan?' asked Appu.

'I'll tell you when you are a big boy.'

Holding his son's hand, covered with the dripping veils of bogscum in its varied shades, Rajan began to walk. Past the bog, at the stream, he jumped in and washed the colours off his body.

He sat cross-legged on the soft, green grass and opened the papaya packet. The papaya was now fully ripe. Appu sat staring at it.

Rajan took out his pocket-knife and rubbed the rust away on a stone. The sharpened knife shone in the sun. Rajan cut the papaya into three. 'Appu, let this shattered weapon of our revolution be our breakfast.' Appu swallowed hard and smiled.

'This is for you, this for Amma, and this for me,' said Rajan. 'These bunches of flowers, these balls woven from palm leaves, and these playthings of little nuts and palm-leaf ribs are no longer the property of the revolution. They have become just toys once again. They have attained liberation.'

'My fellow revolutionary, robber of trains, may the blessings of the secret whispered by the train be with you forever. May your children always have food for their hunger.'

Rajan wrapped Lakshmi's share of the papaya in the towel, and then listening to his train whistle once more, somewhere in the distance, he · walked on holding his child's hand.

Translated by Ajithan G. Kurup

OBSEQUIES FOR THE LIVING

C.V. SREERAMAN

As he climbed the steps, Akilesh Kumar Sinha said, 'Vishnupada Temple is the most ancient temple of Bharat Varsha. It was here that Prince Siddhartha sought refuge after he sacrificed everything.'

'He walked a little further along the banks of this river. At last, under the shade of the bodhi tree . . .' said the person behind Sinha.

Sinha turned around and looked at him. 'Haran,' he said, 'I was looking for you.'

'Haran Panda,' Sinha introduced him to me and then turned to Panda, 'This is my friend. He has come from far away. He wants to perform the shraddha. Please do everything as it should be done. Don't charge even half a paisa extra.'

Panda agreed to do everything.

'I'll take leave then. Before you leave Gaya you must try to visit my house,' said Sinha to me.

'Please come with me,' said Panda as he walked ahead. 'Do you know Hindi?'

'Yes.'

When we reached the doorway of the temple, Panda said, 'You can leave your slippers here. The chokras will keep them for you — for a small charge, of course . . .'

'I am not wearing slippers.'

Panda looked at my naked feet under the ochre-coloured pyjamas.

We went in. The place was full of people. People speaking many languages, their bodies covered with different kinds of clothes, praying in their own words — with their own needs, their own griefs . . .

'Don't you want to pray?' asked Panda.

'I'll wait till the shraddha is done,' I said.

We walked on, got out of the temple through another doorway and reached the ghat.

'Which river is this? The Ganga?'

'No. But this is also a holy river, the Phalgu. A branch of the Ganga.'

The river was dry. Dull and lifeless. Although it was only eight in the morning, noon overflowed on the dry sands in the middle of the river.

'And what is that on the other side of the river?'

'Those are also temples. Nandigram, Ramgaya, Sitakund. It was there that Rama and Lakshmana performed the obsequies for King Dasaratha. Sita made the pindam* with sand . . .'

We sat down on the concrete bench near the bathing ghat.

'And what is this?'

'Shmashan Ghat.'

No sooner did he say it than a dead body was brought in on a stretcher. Hari bol . . . Hari bol . . . They lowered the stretcher and tried to heap the firewood.

Panda was young, but his eyes were sunken. He had a pale yellow face and eyes. Was it grief, sickness or stark poverty?

He said to me, 'Babu, may I ask you something? Please don't feel bad about it, but . . . have you come to Gaya only for this?'

'Yes.'

'Do you live very far away?'

'About two thousand miles from here.'

'Gadadhar! Hari! Pundarikaksha!' Panda exclaimed to himself. 'Prince Siddhartha came here seeking knowledge and enlightenment — to find answers to the thousand questions that rose within him.'

He continued after a brief silence, 'Babu, you know how many religions found their way to this Magadha. Not one of them could grow

---

pindam: funeral offerings, usually balls of cooked rice

roots here. Our faith . . .'

'Hey Panda, idhar aao,' came the call behind us.

'Coming.' Panda got up and ran.

Like the crows that crowd around the pindam to eat it, a number of pandas* rushed to the spot. Haran Panda was the first to get there. He met a boy running toward him with enthusiasm, a camera hanging around his neck like a flower basket. The boy must have been seven or eight. A young woman followed him. She was fair, with bright eyes and a broad forehead. A fine face, though her hair seemed thin. Her body was well-chiselled, and she walked with her head held high — a little like a man. Her scarf was untied and it hung loose around her neck like that of a boy scout. She had reddish lines on her forehead and cheeks; maybe the scarf had been tied too tight earlier. An uncommonly tall young man, wearing trousers, shirt and tie, was with her. Only his feet were naked. He must have left his shoes behind with the chokras outside the temple. His hair, smeared with cream or vaseline and combed neatly, gleamed in the morning sunlight. They walked towards the ghat with Panda and a few beggar boys.

'I think they are in a hurry,' Panda said to me apologetically. 'I'll send them away soon,' and he hurried after them.

'We come from Cuttack,' began the woman.

Panda interrupted her to say something in Oriya.

'Don't assault the language. Speak in Hindi, Pandaji.' Then she turned to the young man and spoke to him in English. Her pronunciation was excellent. She must have studied in a public school . . . or maybe abroad.

'Mr Ninan, tell him you come from Kottayam. This panda will speak at least two words of your language.'

She turned again to Panda, 'Look here, Panda, we have to be back in Calcutta by five in the evening. There's a company meeting. We have to perform the shraddha of the boy's father. What is the minimum time required?'

---

pandas: priests, usually based in certain parts of North India; they often keep genealogies and maintain a relationship with a network of families

'An hour . . .'

'Impossible. Reduce it.'

'Half an hour.'

'No. Reduce it some more.'

'Fifteen minutes.'

'Ten minutes.'

Panda agreed.

'Ma,' he asked her, 'Is this your child?'

'Yes. Why do you ask?'

'Because I see a resemblance.'

A resemblance! I was surprised. He was dark. He had a very small face. A narrow forehead. Small eyes. What did the Panda mean?

'I see . . . yes,' she conceded.

'Ma . . . did the child's father die in an accident?'

Her face faded and grew pale. She looked at the young man with her.

'Why do you want to know all that?' Her lips too paled as she spoke.

'You are young, so I thought . . .' faltered Panda.

'What does it have to do with performing the obsequies?' she asked, a little irritated.

'You see,' said Panda, 'if it's a case of apaghat mrtyu,* we have to place the pindam on the pretasila* in front of the railway station. That would be best.'

'Mrs Panigrahi, what sort of deaths are called apaghat mrtyu?' the young man asked her in English.

She turned to Panda, 'What sort of deaths?'

'Accidents.'

'What else?'

'Murder.'

'What else?'

'Suicide . . .'

She did not ask 'What else?' Nor did Panda say anything more. She

---

apaghat mrtyu: accidental death

pretasila: a stone representing a dead person for whom the shraddha has not yet been performed; till this is done, the person cannot be liberated from the cycle of life and death was thoughtful for a while, then said to the young man, 'Mr Ninan, they always manage to confuse people.' She bowed her head for a while. Then looking up, she said firmly, 'Let it be done here. Who can climb the hill to the pretasila?'

Panda called the boy. The boy took the camera off his neck and gave it to the young man. 'Uncle Ninan, one roll of film while I perform the shraddha. Use up one roll,' said the boy in impeccable English. He must study in some posh school.

'What is your caste?' Panda asked the woman.

'Brahmin.'

'Do you eat rice or wheat?'

'Rice.'

'So the pindam must be rice?'

'Yes,' replied the woman.

'Rice will take longer to cook. Impossible in the time fixed.'

'Then use wheat,' she declared.

Panda called to the boy, 'What's your name?'

'Chittaranjan Panigrahi.'

'Go have a bath first.'

'Where?'

'Here, in this water. In this holy river . . . the pure water of the Phalgu.'

The lowest step dug into the sand. The water reached the boy's ankle.

'In this water full of weeds?' asked the woman, staring at Panda.

'Not if you don't want him to . . . but let him sprinkle some water on his head.'

'Come on.'

The boy rolled up his jeans and walked down the steps.

She called aloud, 'Be careful, a little water will do. Or you will catch a cold.'

The boy sprinkled a few drops of water on his head, jumped up two steps at a time, and paused to ask, 'What do you say, Uncle Ninan?'

Uncle Ninan clapped his hands. The boy climbed up the steps, two

at a time, saying 'Up . . . up . . .' The beggar boys also followed two
steps at a time. Uncle Ninan continued to clap. The woman watched
the muscles on his forearm with a smile on her lips.

Panda had rolled the cooked wheat into balls. 'Sit down,' he said.

The boy sat facing Panda.

'Put on this pavitra . . . show me your finger.' Panda slipped the ring
made of darbha grass onto his finger.

'Roll the wheat into balls when I tell you to.'

'Uncle Ninan, one snap please . . .'

'Yes, Mr Ninan, go ahead,' the woman said.

Ninan took a photo. Then he spread a copy of the *Amrita Bazaar
Patrika* on the steps and sat down. She sat very close to him as if they
had been living like this for a long time. But when he looked at her she
blushed and withdrew her eyes shyly. Like two people not yet familiar
with each other.

'How hot it is!' he said to her. 'There's not even a leaf to shade the
car where we have parked it. The beer bottles inside may boil — and I
don't know what they will turn into.'

'Mr Ninan, do you think we can reach Calcutta by six? The Board of
Directors meets at seven.'

'So what if we don't make it? You and I are here. Mr Sohan Pradhan
is in hospital. They won't have a quorum.'

'Quorum! Nonsense! I'm not worried about that. When they are all
together, what will they discuss? Us!'

Panda dictated and the boy repeated with something like glee,

'Gaya yam'
'Gaya yam'
'Gaya sire'
'Gaya sire'
'Kolahal parvate'
'Kolahal parvate'
'Magadha deshe'
'Magadha deshe'

She sat there, her eyes on the dry bed of the river. Then she muttered,

'There's only one question I can't answer. The Cuttack Medical College was only thirty miles away. There were two cars in the shed . . . then why the local dispensary . . .' and she stopped abruptly.

'Of late,' he told her, 'people say you were not even in the house.'

'Oh God! What stories one has to listen to!'

'Before that we . . . we did it . . . only once . . .'

'No,' she insisted. 'Twice.'

'No, only once. I'm sure.'

'Twice . . . I can bet on it.'

'Then tell me, when was the second time?'

'I will,' she said, as she untied and bit the tangled darbha grass someone had thrown away after performing the rites. 'Wasn't it the morning when your wife was admitted to the mental hospital for the first time? You told me your body was trembling. We went to the Gymkhana Club and woke up the steward. You had drunk a lot of country liquor, without even brushing your teeth . . .'

'I remember now . . . it was between the curtains of the stage at the Club.'

'On the bare dusty floor . . .' she halted, flushing.

He took the blade of darbha grass from her hand and drew on her forearm with it, 'Everything is so green in your memory!'

'It was eight or nine years ago.'

'No,' he said. 'It's been eight years since I came back from the States . . . seven since I joined your coal mines.' He paused. 'What great hopes I came with! Your company has made progress but personally it has not made much difference to me.'

'Don't be silly. After all, tomorrow is ours,' she said, pulling at his tie.

'Pretanam'

'Pretanam'

'Mukhavasanartham'

The boy's voice faltered; his words were no longer clear. Then he stopped altogether, and cried aloud as if a dam had burst.

'Chitho,' she called as she got up and rushed to him. 'Chitho,' she called again and said something to him in Oriya.

The boy opened his eyes. A tear glimmered, stuck to his eyelashes before it jerked free and trickled down, and then there was a torrent of tears down his cheeks.

'Stop, Panda. The boy's crying. Let him stop crying.'

The boy stared at her with bloodshot eyes and yelled, 'Go away.'

She looked at him without batting an eyelid — as if she were staring at a stranger. Or perhaps, at a face too familiar, a face she was tired of.

The young man got up and went to them. 'Don't cry. Uncle Ninan will take your photograph. Come on, please smile.'

'Panda, why did the boy cry? What did you say?' she asked him gently though she seemed angry.

'Thakur Ma, I didn't say anything offensive. All I said was: Your father's soul, hungry and thirsty, has reached this step.'

'This step?' she repeated, and stepped back immediately.

'Please smile,' said Uncle Ninan, bending forward with the camera.

The boy flared up. 'Go away!' He picked up a ball of wheat and threw it at him. The man did not expect this, and didn't try to duck it either. The wheat flour stuck to his face. He was not angry, but his face filled with fear. He went back to the newspaper spread on the steps.

'Continue,' said the boy to Panda in a tone of authority.

'Pretanam'

'Pretanam'

'Mukhavasanartham'

'Mukhavasanartham'

'Thambulam'

'Thambulam'

'Aham'

'Aham'

'Diyate'

'Diyate'

'Upadishtata'

'Upadishtata'

Panda went on in his metallic voice. The boy repeated the words in a quivering tone.

She walked away to where he sat on the newspaper. She tried to sit near him, but to her surprise, her knees wouldn't bend. So she walked instead to the wall of the temple and stood at the foot of the fig tree, watching everything intently.

A body was in flames on the cremation ground. The people who had come with it were impatiently waiting for it all to be over.

'Andhatamo nivaranartham'

'Andhatamo nivaranartham'

Panda made the boy recite after him.

'Deepam'

'Deepam'

'Aham diyate'

'Aham diyate'

She looked on, embarrassed, at the obsequies being performed here against her will. She watched it all — her own rites — helplessly. Rites for her living self.

Panda got up. So did the boy. They circumambulated.

Panda walked down the steps, the boy following him.

The pindam was floated down the Phalgu. The boy broke into heart-rending sobs as though he had lost something. He collapsed into Panda's arms. Panda wiped his tears with his dirty towel smeared with sweat and grime.

She opened her handbag and gave Panda his dakshina. Perhaps it was more than what he had expected. He took it, smiled and joined his palms together. He did not argue about the amount.

'Thakur Ma, wasn't the dead one a brahmin? It's best to have three brahmins sit where the obsequies were performed and recite the Vishnu-sahasranam.'*

'There's no time for all that.'

'Thakur Ma can go. If you give them the dakshina, I will make them recite it.'

Vishnusahasranam: the thousand names of Vishnu

'Call them.'

Panda clapped his hands and three people came running immediately. One was an old man with elephantiasis; another a middle-aged one with a pock-marked face and a squint-eye; and the third a young man with sandal paste smeared on his earlobes.

She spoke to them directly, 'You are to sit here and recite the Vishnusahasranam thrice. What's your fee?'

'Five rupees each.'

'I'll give you three rupees each,' she said, opening her bag and taking out a bundle of one-rupee notes. She pulled out a steel hairpin from her hair and prised open the staple holding the currency notes together with a nail-cutter from her bag and counted out a few notes. She counted them again and then once again before she gave three rupees to each.

'I say to you on the steps of this holy temple: You should recite the Sahasranam thrice.'

'Yes, we will.'

'We are brahmins. Will you keep your word?'

'Of course. Bhagwan kasam.'

The boy no longer sobbed. But his face was still pale and he hiccupped now and then.

They walked away. The boy walked ahead, she followed. The young man was behind them. They disappeared behind the walls of the Vishnupada temple.

The brahmins spread their towels and sat down. '*Om namo bhagavate vasudevaya* . . .' they recited, without rhythm, in crude voices that swallowed their words.

'*Avyaya Purushaha Sakshi . . .*'

The old man yawned once or twice. He lit a beedi and began to smoke.

'Sali! What does she think we are, idiots?' He spat into the ghat, abusing her at the end of every sentence. The others continued their recitation. Then the squint-eyed one paused to put some ground tobacco into his mouth before he joined in the cacophony again. His tobacco soaked in his saliva and the corners of his mouth were streaked red.

'*Brahmanyo brahmakrit Brahma Brahma* . . . ' he sneezed. Coughed. Then stopped.

The deep eyes of the young man were set hard in meditation. His voice was only just turning masculine. He seemed to have forgotten everything around him. He continued to recite,

'*Aparajita sarvaseho*
niyanta niyamo yama
Satvavan satvika satya
satya dharma parayana.'

His voice went on and on, without halting, on the steps of Gaya — till the end of time; firm, unceasing, like an insatiable craving for knowledge.

Translated by B. Chandrika

THE GODDESSES OF ARSHABHARATA

MANASY

I was the wife of a respectable, affluent officer of Arshabharata, the land of rishis and sages. A lucky woman with a huge house, a car and all other pleasures, I sometimes think to myself. I often sit for a long time gazing at my reflection in the large rosewood dining-table. Looking out, I can see the poor women bringing water in the scorching heat, in their disfigured aluminium vessels. Their children hang in bundles on their backs. The singular expression on their faces, which remains unchanged even after constant washing, reminds me of stained coins of little value. I do not know what to do with these coins. I cannot throw them away. After all, it is money. So I put them back into my mind.

The women of Arshabharata are respectable, Amma would say. That's why men call us devis and worship us. And forget that we have hunger and thirst like human beings. It's a pity, we could have all been devis. The mistake is to continue being human amid those ready to make us devis.

Lying beside my husband, listening to his light breathing, I always remember Amma's words. A man with wealth and a bright future at his feet, I wonder why he married me? I agree with him when he says that a woman is a burden. I knew it when I saw my father's forced smile and anxious face every time those who came with offers of marriage assessed me, looking at my face, breasts and waist. I remember his frustration when somebody once left with the remark, 'The girl is okay, but she is dark.' Enraged, he threw away the food laid on the table and walked upstairs with heavy footsteps. My father's face looms large in my mind, turning all my desires into a mirage. I then look at my husband's face and smile guiltily. I, who have never earned a single paisa, have known the value of money since childhood. Money means a pair of wings and a mind of one's own. I have always felt grateful to men for feeding us and clothing us in exchange for our clipped wings and faded, soiled minds. They cover us with pretty clothes and jewels, and adorn our foreheads with blood-red kumkumam, making us respectable. They hold our hands tight and take us along with them. In such moments, we have to smile. I can see that the clipped wings add to our splendour. Shouldn't women too be thankful?

When we are worshipped in our houses, when we are devis with large eyes, beautiful nose and full breasts, complaints, and even requests, are superfluous. What do you expect from men? That is why I am able to understand Lalaji's sorrow — Lalaji who married a second and third time to get a son. I too had gone to Lalaji's third wedding. He shook my husband's hand happily and proudly. Later, he stroked his grey hair with a hand which glittered with a diamond ring as he lamented, 'Look, this is the third time I am trying my luck. My only prayer to God is to shower mercy on me at least this time. Mr Nair, I am growing old. It is inauspicious to have women reigning in the family.'

Lalaji's first wife, the mother of three grown-up girls, held the bride's hand and led her. Their eyes met through the thin, red, beautifully embroidered veil. The bride stared at the smile of her predecessor, a smile like the dimmed light of a soot-filled lantern. All of a sudden she seemed to realise the weight of the heavy responsibility placed on her. She never smiled again. Lalaji's second wife stood still, near the large dishes of food, with all the keys of the house bound around her waist. The guests and the bride who had come to give Lalaji a son walked to the bridal chamber. The eyes of the elder wives shone in the never-brightening darkness of the kitchen, like granite splinters. I thought a fire would blaze and burn if they were rubbed against anything, or if they touched each other. I sat near them, arranging the paper plates and napkins. Lalu, the second wife, threw pots and pans about in her anger. She made a lot of noise opening and closing cupboards and drawers. Suddenly she burst into tears and her face was completely wet. I sat silent, stroking her trembling shoulders.

'Amma must have come,' the eldest wife got up in a hurry and shut the door. Then she chided the younger one, 'Crying on the day of your husband's marriage? What is wrong with you?' She wanted to say more. But she stopped herself and turned away. Her lips trembled like the sudden glowing flame of burning firewood. Pretending this was the beginning of a smile, she looked at me as if she was going to complete it. But the smile did not grow.

I left Lalaji's house that day holding my husband's hand. I looked back at the faces which had been following me like the everlasting scar of a burn caused unknowingly, and thought: What Lalaji said was true. If we don't have men in every generation, all of them growing up with prowess, who else can we have for support? The girl Veena who comes to work in my house, with her fifteen-day-old baby in a bundle on her back, will also understand this. Her husband basks in the sun all day, smoking his hookah. To be secure, she has to pay the price for his health and happiness. Guards are important for those of us who always live in fear and guilt.

One day, Veena came to work without the baby on her back.

'Where is your son?' I asked. She stared at me with her large, dry eyes. I saw the milk oozing out from her big breasts and wetting her dirty blouse.

'My husband took him away,' Veena said. 'After all the baby is his! We women don't even own our children. But memsaab,' she continued, 'the child is burning with fever. I sat outside the house all night listening to the child cry. I thought I'd ask my husband to forgive me when he came out to wash his face. I could go into the house then. Doesn't he too have a heart? Doesn't he know that the child will be thirsty? Nothing happened. Finally, when he came out with the child, I followed him, crying aloud. The baby had closed his eyes, and he couldn't even cry. I was weeping, and this made my husband even more angry. He said he would throw the child into the gutter if I followed him. I know his temper, I knew he would not hesitate to do it. Buy him something quickly, I said, he's thirsty. And I stood there till they disappeared beyond the hut and the fence. I stood there till I had to come here. Memsaab, why did God create women? He could have created just men.'

Veena told me all this as if she was narrating a story. Suddenly she stopped as if she saw God right in front of her. Later she sat in a corner of my room and began to cry. I saw that her blouse was stained with milk and that her face was wet with tears. The milk and tears covered me with small ripples which then became suffocating waves.

'Veena, shall I give you some tea?' I finally asked. I had nothing else to say. She shook her head and squeezed the milk from her aching, hardened breasts into a glass.

When I saw this I called out to God helplessly, though I did not have the faintest idea of the god I was calling. I pleaded, 'We will give you all the wings we have if you need them. Give back Veena her child.'

God had always been a stranger to me, as he was today. But I did not believe in calling out and crying to anybody visible. So I addressed my futile calls to an invisible god. Veena's milk and tears gradually dried up, like water absorbed by iron. She bore the weight of pent-up, dried milk and hardened tears. She became all-suffering like Mother Earth.

'*Kshamaya dharitri* — in patience like Mother Earth — says the scripture,' I once told Veena. 'Men are human, with anger, lust and desire. All of us ought to be devis. Veena, men are born as human beings and die human beings. We are born human but we have to live like devis.'

Veena, who was cleaning her toe-nail with a broomstick, nodded.

'I just wanted to see him once,' she said. 'He must have started walking. He will not recognize me now. He'll cry loudly when I hold him.'

Looking at my reflection on the shining table, I felt that it is all true. As grandmother says, all of us should be Seelavathis.* Our husbands' wishes should be ours too. Otherwise, what will we do outside their doors if they discard us? If I sit on the pavement with nothing except the clothes I have on, and a fading vermilion mark on my forehead, I

Seelavathi: idealised in Indian mythology as the paragon of chastity

will be jeered at. Underneath a sun which burns like a funeral pyre, amid all this hustle, from whom can I beg for food? If some god does not reward my chastity with an akshayapatram,* or a boon that grants me all my wishes, I would be in a pitiable state. Yes, it is better to have a permanent abode to live and beg in.

I felt, once more, an increasing respect for my husband, and my devotion to him grew. Here I accept with open hands the secure shade above me and all these pleasures around me. But I have nothing to give in return, except some love as clear and transparent as tears. But I do not give love to get anything in return. I would literally collapse if I start giving away this too, the only possession I have, in exchange for something else. I will not have anything of my own then, when I look out on the world from my window, oblivious of everything. As my husband once remarked, loving too is a kind of selfishness. I love for my own happiness. Then what else shall I sell? My liabilities suffocate me like a wave that shrouds everything. These liabilities will remain even after three births. If my husband were not as rich as he is, if my saris and house were not as expensive as they are, my liabilities might have dwindled a little. Then I realised that they were actually growing, becoming limitless. I realised, as if suddenly enlightened, why a woman should have patience. She has to be grateful for everything around her, even her children. I felt ashamed at the thought that I had to live so long to realise these simple truths. That was how I gave away my mind and wings, the symbols of my humanness, in exchange for the turmeric and vermilion, the remnants of offerings. That was how I became a devi, with eyelashes that no longer flicker, and lips that no longer quiver, like any other woman of Arshabharata.

Translated by Usha Nambudripad

---

akshayapatram: a mythical vessel with an inexhaustible supply of food

THE KAYASTHAS

ANAND

Mathematics was never a subject of numbers alone. A problem does not end at the point where a teacher of mathematics examines it and declares it right or wrong. The questions the problem raised continue to exist. The events which led to its construction also took place long before the master of numbers came on the scene. If someone tells you that two plus two makes five, this is not necessarily an indication of his ignorance. On the other hand, it could be a sign of his cleverness; that is, if he is trying to trick you. What I mean is that mistakes do not just happen; they are committed too. An intelligent man often distorts facts for his benefit. I use the word intelligent deliberately. There is even a school of thought that says human civilisation was born at the moment when man began to lie.

Let me get back to the subject. I was trying to tell you that there are so many things which apparently do not relate to numbers, lying beyond the two points within which a problem manifests itself before us with mathematical dimensions. Among these countless facts, meshed together, criss-crossing, the idea of mathematics is sometimes lit up; sometimes the idea of morality, sometimes reason, sometimes justice. You know, we use the very same words, right and wrong, when we handle any of these subjects and exercise our judgment. And these words indicate a variety of judgments, depending on situation and disposition; they can be used to mean good and bad, dharma and adharma, just and unjust, what can be done and what should not be done.

But using the same words to denote these various aspects of our experience does not mean that we behave in the same way when dealing with each one of them. For example, a teacher in mathematics examines his student's exercise and gives him five marks if he has done it right, and zero if it is wrong. But a magistrate lets off the accused if he finds he has done the right thing; and packs him off to jail if he was wrong. In the first case, the right-doer gets a reward and the wrong-doer goes empty-handed; in the second, it is the right-doer who goes empty-handed, with the wrong-doer getting punished. See, even though these two people have more or less the same conception of right and wrong, how differently they behave?

I was trying to tell you that things like mathematics, science, morality, dharma and justice do not exactly have independent existences. A mathematician cannot plead that he has nothing to do with the questions of dharma; he cannot look the other way while they confront him. A scientist cannot argue that he is not interested in matters of morality, nor can a moralist pretend that he can rely on intuition alone. And yet something divides all these. Such divisions have sometimes isolated each completely, and put them in watertight compartments with the argument that every discipline should maintain its independence and purity. Sometimes, if this segregation is not insisted upon, a different approach is suggested for each case; two approaches as different as in the case of the teacher and the magistrate!

How and when all this happened is difficult to say. There is perhaps no acceptable definition for what we mean by truth. That is why man continues to pursue the truth. The wise say that if you cannot perceive the aim clearly, be sure of your means at least. But the question is, how do you cut the road without knowing the destination? The more we think, the more entangled we are in arguments. Good logicians can always escape pitfalls with the skill of their tongues.

I am trying here to see if I can shed a ray of light on a scene which is, as I have already warned you, deeply murky. I believe the history of the scribes and accountants of our society may be of some help. You know, we had a class of people among us who made record-keeping and accountancy their exclusive profession. Tradition called them kayasthas. The British rulers appointed them to keep the accounts of their colonial government. Before the British, the kayasthas kept accounts for the Mughals, the Guptas, the Rashtrakutas, the Pushyabhutis, the Chalukyas, the Sakas and who knows who else. In a way, we can say that these people began the system of public accounting in our country.

The kayasthas do not figure in the chaturvarnya. So they were not born out of any part of Vishnu's body. Then what was their origin? There is a stanza in the Vishnu Purana which says that Chitragupta came out of Brahma with an ink bottle in one hand and a pen in the other. But this could have been a piece added by someone later on, after these people were established in their jobs with ink bottles and pens. In fact, the kayasthas most probably came to India from the north, across the Himalayas, perhaps from Persia. The Vishnudharmottara Purana calls them udichyas. Unlike the Indians, they wear trousers and jackets, we are told. The first such figure we encounter in history, the first reference to a man with an ink bottle and a pen, is that of Dandi. Dandi sits beside Surya, the prime historian, on a seat of lotus in the famous time chariot, with his tools, the bottle and pen. We know that Surya had a brother, Mitra, who lived in Persia. Mitra, the other son of Kashyapa Prajapati, was a favourite of the Persians. Considering all this, we can perhaps deduce that Mitra sent Dandi to assist Surya in the stupendous task he was carrying out.

So our story begins at the point when, after crossing deserts, snowy mountains and turbulent rivers, Dandi the northerner finally arrived one day before Surya. Men had just become aware of the phenomena of time and history. The Sindhu and Ganga valleys were agog with the activities that constitute civilization: agriculture, town-building, trade and war. Through all this, Surya drove his chariot that was pulled by seven horses and supported by a single wheel. Wherever his chariot passed, people woke up and paid their respects to him. The moment he left, darkness took hold of the world and they fell asleep again. Where there was Surya, there history was lit up. Surya saw everything, witnessed everything. Thus Surya became the first historian of the earth; the wheel of his chariot was called the wheel of time. As that wheel rolled, hours, days, seasons, years and ages came alive; the world broke its monotony to enter the era of events.

Dandi stood spellbound at the sight of the awe-inspiring journey of this chariot. But soon his face darkened with sadness. Surya asked Dandi the cause of his unhappiness.

Dandi said: 'My lord, you are the omnipresent; the witness of all. Nothing escapes your eyes. The seven horses which pull your chariot are the seven metres which convert sounds into words and ideas. Yet what you see goes unrecorded. How can this be so?'

Was this strange-looking person sent by his brother in the north telling him that his life had been an exercise in futility? But in the words of this man, which at first seemed to be plain arrogance, Surya discovered a gentle warning. Perhaps his brother wanted to tell him through this messenger: My dear brother, you are elated by the fact that you are the father historian. But events do not become history by themselves; they are to be recorded and remembered.

Surya did not hesitate any longer. He drew Dandi into his chariot and gave him the seat to his right. Dandi became his record-keeper, the first chronicler of the first historian.

Pingala, who sat to the left of Surya, commanded the horses. He was their navigator; he knew all the routes and distances. At the crossing of every constellation, he cautioned his lord. At makara rasi,* he announced the advent of uttarayana, and at mithuna rasi, the advent of dakshinayana. Dandi recorded everything, the account of every equinox, month, day, hour and even seconds. Nothing escaped the sharp point of his pen which hunted down every event that occurred on the earth. Every time the chariot crossed the equator and when day and night were equal in length, Dandi closed the accounts and stitched the records of the past six months into a volume and pushed it to the back of the chariot.

As the chariot of Surya rolled on, the reins of Pingala made waves in the air, and the mighty pen of Dandi wove patterns of numbers in his

---

Makara rasi and mithuna rasi are signs of the Hindu zodiac; makara is the equivalent of Cancer and mithuna of Gemini. The year is divided into uttarayana and dakshinayana according to the relative positions of the sun and the earth.

book; and the history of the world strode ahead. Pingala was thrilled by the sight of passing constellations and changing equinoxes. Dandi drowned himself in the exciting sea of figures. The rumblings of the chariot's single wheel, and the hooves of the galloping horses, provided the music of inspiration to them.

But not everything was music on the earth. The lives of men travelled the rugged path of pleasure and sorrow. Fortune and misfortune, virtue and sin, justice and injustice, compassion and cruelty, haunted them. Neither Surya nor his assistants on either side noticed that. Their eyes remained on the movement of the chariot. For these three people, time was history and history was chronicling. But something was going wrong somewhere between history and life. The first indication we get of this is from Samjna, the wife of Surya. Samjna was the daughter of Viswakarma, who built the chariot for Surya. In keeping with her name, Samjna liked to examine the specifics of everything. She knew every shape and shade; she never wanted to let anything remain vague; or to be left to chance. Under what circumstances the marriage between Surya and Samjna was consummated we do not know, but the Mahabharata says a great deal about their marriage which ended in a tragic separation. Surely Viswakarma must have warned his daughter about Surya!

'Dear one, this man rides a chariot with one wheel. Motion alone keeps him in balance. He can visualise only one dimension. He perceives no peculiarities, does not recognise one thing apart from the other. He looks neither left nor right, like a horse with its eyes covered on both sides, as he rides ahead in his chariot.'

This marriage between the abstract and the concrete could be one of the preordained destinies of history. It led to the birth of a son, Yamadharma. Immediately after Yama was born, Samjna, who had already found it impossible to get along with her husband, left Surya and her son. She went to the forest and into the oblivion of history. The one-dimensioned Surya did not even notice. According to the Vishnu Purana, he mistook Samjna's maid Chhaya for his wife, and took her into his arms.

The unfortunate child, Yama, was the tragic result of this broken marriage. He grew up like a question mark hanging between the abstract and the precise, between history and life. He could not understand why this sadness swelled up within him. He would stand watching his grandfather Viswakarma moulding the endless ideas that flowed out of his mind into sculptures and structures. If he asked the old man something, he would only smile. The restless child would jump into his father's chariot. But Surya, the witness of all, had no time to talk to him.

Yama grew more and more lonely. He wandered alone in the cities that simmered with life, and in the quiet pastures where nothing ever seemed to happen. And then, lo, he saw a boy in the shadow of a huge rock, with an ink bottle, a pen and some writing materials by him. The anguish on his face drew Yama towards him. 'Who are you angry with?' asked Yama as he went up to him.

'Anger seems to have disappeared from this world,' the boy raised his head and mumbled. 'Either there is quiet resignation or cold cruelty everywhere. Sorrow and anger are left only in you and me, my friend.'

'How can you see what is going on in me?'

'Come here to the shade of this rock,' invited the boy. 'Come away from that cruel sun.'

Yama looked up towards Surya.

'Yes, they are great people, our fathers,' the boy continued. 'But they cannot contain us. That is why we are their children. We came out of them to travel beyond them. I am Chitragupta, son of Dandi who sits by your father's side in his chariot and notes the progress of time.'

Yama came forward eagerly and took Chitragupta in his arms.

Slowly Chitragupta unfolded his story before Yama. The days spent in thought and the arguments with himself. The long discourses he had with his father Dandi. And how he had ultimately left his house to come to this wilderness.

He had grown up in the company of ink pots and pens, among volumes of books. With no friends other than figures and letters. But the more he learned the mathematics of his father, and the more he read the history written by his father, the more he revolted against them.

'What good are these accounts to us, father? The long accounts of seasons, solstices, years and ages, which recur in the same fashion, one after another. What are we going to do with them?' asked the boy Chitragupta one day.

'This is history, my son,' Dandi earnestly replied. 'There is no escaping it. Nor do we have a choice. It has been my privilege to record it. And I have been doing it without overlooking even a single moment. Whatever system you adopt to measure it, there will be no mistake in my accounts. You can add its columns vertically or horizontally; they will always tally.'

'Father, mathematics is not just the addition and subtraction of numbers. It is an attempt to discover what is right; the rights and the wrongs too. What happens in this world, how many deceptions, betrayals, frauds, treacheries, cruelties, sins, evils . . .'

Dandi smiled, 'You do not know, my dear, there is not a single event that has taken place that is not recorded in my books.'

Chitragupta shook his head. 'Events do not exist by themselves in this world, father, they have characters too.'

'Do you think the great Surya who sees every event does not see their characters too? Surya is witness of all, Chitragupta.'

'With witnesses alone, can a court function, can you dispense justice, father? You need witnesses, and you also need the complainants, the judge and the person who executes the judgment . . .'

Dandi felt uneasy. He said, 'We are kayasthas, just clerks, my dear one. Our instruments are ink and pen, not sword and shield. It is enough for us to move our pens. Move them along with the times. Go with the times. Serve the times . . .'

Chitragupta said to Yama, 'Son of Surya, the world has many seekers of truth. Saints, scientists, mathematicians, architects . . . all move because of the fire within them. But all these people pursue just one aim they have selected. They turn away from all other truths and facts. Thus they miss the total and larger truth. And when they pursue that single small truth, they close their eyes to a large number of falsehoods which surround and suffocate it. So not only do they mutilate the totality of truth, but also allow the little truth which they pursue to be imprisoned by the untruth around it. The pen is powerful, my father told me. But when we cut out the truth from its environment and put it in a cage as a show-piece, when we move with the times without protest, then the pen turns out to be a mere stick. I was not ready to accept that situation. I left my house and came to the shelter of this rock . . . Sitting here, I began writing my own accounts sheet.' He paused a moment and then continued sadly, 'Yet, son of Surya, my accounts too are only accounts. I have no power to put them into operation. I too am only a kayastha, a clerk.'

'Friend,' said Yama, a lump in his throat. 'My father is Surya. He can see everything. My mother Samjna is the mother of classification and concrete detail. My grandfather can give shape to any kind of complex idea. And yet all these people did was to give me this pain and send me out into the world. Only you have made me see the reason for the pain I carry. I will not allow your anger to end up as yet another pain. Come, let us get on with our task to connect mathematics with justice. To merge science and morality into one. Our subject is not dry statistics, it is life in its wholeness.'

The path Yama and Chitragupta took was not smooth. It is not easy to write down statements of accounts on the paper of morality. Or to give knowledge the weapons of ideals so that it can be put to use. The perpetrators of injustice laughed at them. Those who wielded power hated them. Even the well-meaning, when under pressure, tried to tempt them and divert them from carrying out justice. The court they established, called Samyamani, was subjected to repeated attacks.

Yama the child, neglected by his father and abandoned by his mother, used to be scolded by the maid Chhaya for his stubbornness. Now he got nothing but curses from every corner. A saint called Animandavya was so incensed with him that he wanted to banish him. Siva, in one of his usual spurts of rage, tried to burn him. But the movement Yama and Chitragupta began was not to be killed. Challenging opposition, facing obstructions, failing and succeeding, destroyed and resurrected, the dispensation of dharma continued.

What was intended to integrate actually ended up, as usual, with fragmentation. The traditional school of kayasthas did not agree with Chitragupta and his disciples. They withdrew deeper and deeper into the shells of their conventions. Thus began the usual course of mutual allegations, expulsions and ostracism. The scribes ultimately split into two sects: those who followed the path of time and those who took to the path of dharma. In the name of purity, the time-kayasthas restricted themselves to maintaining the accounts of events and happenings. They came to be known as grama kayasthas and grama dwivaras during the time of Kalhana; they later assumed various other positions — patwaris, lipikars and accountants. They moved with the times easily and without any mental conflict. They served those who were in power every time — Yavanas, Sakas, Hunas, Mughals, the British and ultimately the despots of their own colour. They maintained the account books for all of them. In their registers, the columns of receipts and issues always cancelled each other to leave zero in the end. Hiuen-Tsang onwards, all the great travellers who visited the country praised them. From Dandi, who sat by the side of Surya on a lotus flower, down his numerous descendants, each one of the clan and lineage was described as handsome, brilliant and learned. They made offerings to the ink pot and pen that was kept on a pedestal covered with flowers; and celebrated this auspicious day on the second day of the waning moon in the Chaitra month.

The dharma-kayasthas also worshipped the ink pot and pen, but on the second day of the waxing moon in the month of Kartik. But neither their ink nor their pen could take their accounts to zero. There was always something short or more. Their eyes meticulously caught errors wherever they existed. No ruler could bring them under his control. No one spoke well of them. Eyes deep as wells, teeth sprouting like horns, an aquiline nose, thirty-two hands, each three miles long, a voice like thunder and weapons like lightning — this is how Chitragupta appears in the Brihannaradiya Purana. The Garuda Purana claims that various kinds of scourges permanently camp around Samyamani, the abode of Chitragupta in Yamapuri. The Usana Samhita condemns the whole lot of dharma-kayasthas as wicked and evil.

In short, we are still not prepared to instil dharma in the times. Our civilization has consistently insisted that principles, imagination and sentiments be kept apart. Our capabilities incline more and more towards disintegration, not integration. And so we separate accounts from audit. The executive arm is severed from the judiciary; quantity and quality are made to appear entirely different. Politics has been moved away from morality; technology from science. Development is a stranger to environment. When millions were burnt to death by the atom bomb, we praised the light of a thousand suns rising at a time. After a plane crash which threw hundreds of lives into the sea, we were preoccupied with the excitement and thrill of sending robots to pick up the black box from the ocean's depths.

When did we begin to eulogize the mathematician while locking up reason in the box? When did we learn to worship the politician and hate the judge? When did we decide to approach those who did right and those who did wrong in different ways? I do not know this. The puranas contain lavish passages about worshipping Siva who showers erratic boons, and fearing Yama who carries out justice. Perhaps the whole system of puranas, literature and the arts appeared at this point of our civilization.

Translated by the author

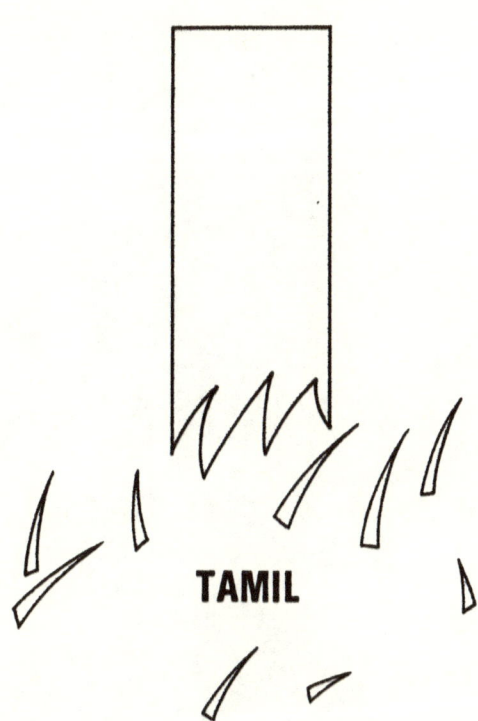

TAMIL

INTRODUCTION

While the first Tamil novel was written a hundred and thirteen years ago, the first Tamil short story is about eighty years old. This form had to wait another twenty years to gain widespread recognition as a valid genre of creative writing, in a language canopied by a tall and wide literary tradition of twenty centuries and more. The history of the Tamil short story really begins with V.V.S. Aiyer's collection entitled *Kulathankarai Arasamaram* (The peepal tree by the pond). As has been the case in the other Indian languages, this first effort was an ambitious, well-crafted and well-executed one.

It was in the 1930s that the genre really blossomed. Unlike the novel, which could straightaway make a book and claim a literary existence all its own, the short story had to depend on what can broadly be called periodical publication, in which is in-built a multiplicity of forces not all conducive to literary pursuits. It is remarkable that some of the finest short stories were written in the nebulous thirties by a few dozen highly educated, enlightened and motivated young people who must also have made up the main readership for the stories produced. Almost all of them were nationalists, and considered Gandhi a supreme leader, a guide and arbiter of right and wrong. Gandhi, his nation-wide movements, the freedom struggle and the like do not feature too frequently in the Tamil novel, and when featured at all they are only a weak presence. But not so in the short story. The Tamil short story has been a considerable force in the dissemination of both ideas and information about the important concerns of the times.

As a natural next step to the growth of short literary creations, anthologies were compiled; and there are quite a few anthologies of Tamil short stories even from those times. Tamil stories in English translation have been making an appearance since independence, and naturally there should be anthologies of these translations also.

Anthologies are not just pre-tested reading material, but also consensus indices of which writers were meaningful to most anthologists and who were the writers who stood the test of time; and of course, they also provide evidence of the shifts and modifications in the values of the society concerned. The writers who appear repeatedly in different anthologies can be seen as the most significant in the language. It is not out of place to mention the names of some of those who wrote the important short stories: Subramanya Bharati, Pudumaipitthan, N. Pitchamurthy, Kaa Naa Subramanyam, Chidambara Subramanian, Rajaji, Mowni, B.S. Ramaiah and, of course, V.V.S. Aiyer. Many of them belong to what is now identified as the Manikkodi Group. *Manikkodi* was the name of a periodical which came out in three spells with three different editors, providing alternate and challenging reading material to what was found in the more established, financially better-supported popular publications then epitomized in *Ananda Vikatan*.

Ananda Vikatan was stewarded by the able and versatile R. Krishnamurthi who also wrote fiction under the pseudonym 'Kalki.' Kalki took modernity, reform and reasonably intelligent writing to people hitherto unaccustomed to any reading at all. Some blame him for making simplistic, entertainment-oriented writing the staple diet of Tamil readers, but in retrospect one finds that Kalki did not fail to offer subtler aspects of fiction also; and he adhered consistently to values of unquestionable wholesomeness. If an anthology of the best Tamil short stories were to be compiled today, almost all the Manikkodi writers would find a place in it, and so would Kalki, who in his times was thought to be the antithesis of Manikkodi, i.e. serious, literary writing.

Ironically, periodical publication, upon which the Tamil short story depended so heavily, let it down in the post-independence years. The periodicals had to become accessible to new generations of neo-literates and also had to be very conscious of circulation. So in the years of galloping readership and advancement in quality and speed of printing, the 1950s and 1960s, the short-story form marked by some amount of seriousness and literary aspiration became an unusable, unsaleable creation. Kaa Naa Subramanyam, who functioned as some kind of sentinel for modern Tamil writing from the 1930s to 1988, the year of his death, could pick just two writers for special mention in the period 1950-1970: Jayakanthan and Sundara Ramaswamy. The two are among us today; all their works are also in print and so available for scrutiny to a student of literature. But this was also the period when T. Janakiraman and Laa Saa Ramamirtham were establishing themselves as those who would carry forward the Manikkodi tradition.

The 1970s and 1980s witnessed some changes. It is true that more and more large-circulation magazines came into existence; and it is also true that idealism of any kind was getting to be inconvenient and even irrelevant. If compromises and adjustments and increased malleability could be the guiding principles for people of more powerful, influential and consequential walks of life, why shouldn't a writer take a little step this side or that? The 1970s saw a boom of 'little' magazines. These were very different from *Manikkodi*. Those who brought out these magazines were much more worldly by this time; they were not subject to the influence of reading material from other languages, notably English; and they had better financial resources. The development of all-Tamil education and increased economic potential gave these 'little' magazines a thoroughly utilitarian base. Each published material from among its own group and mauled the 'enemies' of its own choice and definition. In the crossfire, a few nice things happened: a handful of good writers emerged.

Kandasamy, the author of 'Engalloor' ('Our Town'), is one of the first of a generation of writers whose main tool for reading, writing and reflection has been one language, i.e. Tamil. The linguistic division of the country, and the emphasis placed on the language of the soil as the medium of instruction in educational institutions, could not but bring about a shift in creative writing. Far from being handicapped, there are several good writers from among this group; and their writing has a thoroughly indigenous character as well as all the vitality and force of modern writing. Konangi, who is represented in this volume by his story 'Koppammal' ('The Shadow Game'), is one of the more recent entrants. Kandasamy and Konangi write of two different regions of Tamil Nadu with an intimate and intense knowledge of the land and the people.

Though there is a certain leaning towards regionalism, though they employ the language in original styles that do not fit into conventional moulds, their works satisfy as competent modern prose works.

Who would know unless told that Dilip Kumar, the author of 'Kannadi' ('The Mirror'), is a Gujarati who has chosen Tamil as the language of his creative writing? And Thopil Mohamed Meeran, the author of 'Idhai Eppadi Nirutthuvadhu?' ('How Do We Stop This?'), is from a region very close to Kerala, and his sensibility is a blend of Tamil and Malayalam. Like the other three, he is also a 'little' magazine writer; but the chief vehicles of his writings have been publications devoted to news and happenings in his community. It was in 1988 that he came to be known beyond his community to the larger Tamil audience, and how! His novel *Kadalorathu Gramathin Kadhai* (The story of a village by the seashore) went into repeated editions, selling over 20,000 copies. It was prescribed for academic study and has drawn comment from everyone who matters in the Tamil literary scene today. Meeran's work has also widened the Tamil writer's (and reader's) area of experience through his close and honest scrutiny of certain Muslim communities, their lives and aspirations. In this sense, Mohamed Meeran is an important addition to the growing community of Tamil writers.

No anthology is for all times, more so an anthology of short stories. These four stories, though representative and important in themselves, cannot be said to cover the whole range of Tamil experience today. But it must be admitted that they are indicative of four different and significant facets, and that they reveal far more than what is written about them in this brief introduction.

Ashokamitran

OUR TOWN

SA KANDASAMY

A bag in one hand, another holding up shorts that threatened to drop off, Pakkiri slid down the mound and walked down the road between the tamarind trees. A fruit fell on his shoulder, but it was too small to interest him and he crunched it with his foot. Then, looking around to make sure that he was not being observed, he picked up a stone and flung it into the branches of the tamarind tree. Two good-sized fruits fell down. He picked them up, put one in his pocket, and walked on munching the other.

His mother was chasing the hen from the yard. He watched her for a while. She usually went to the fields to help with the sowing and came back only after sunset. But today here she was already. She saw him and called out, 'Pakkiri, quick!' Pakkiri rested his bag on his head, crossed the canal, stomped through the ragged grass, and came running.

As he got closer to his mother, he pulled out his slate from his bag with great urgency.

And said: 'Amma, I'm the only one who got ten out of ten marks in arithmetic. No one else!' She was delighted. She stepped forward and placed a loving hand on his shoulder. She could not read or write, but she kept looking at the numbers that looked like mere squiggles. The boy was ten years old, big for his age.

'Eat quickly, we are going to our place.'

'Fine,' said Pakkiri. He put his slate back in his bag, ran into the house, hung it on a nail, and went to the backyard. He washed himself with water from the big pot under the poovarasu tree, and came back into the house.

On some Saturdays his mother would take him with her to her hometown, her 'place,' which was Kaveripattinam, twelve miles away. They got there by walking along the banks of the Kaveri under the shade of the pungai trees.

Pakkiri's mother set a plate of rice before him as he dried his hands on the tail of his shirt and sat down to eat. She slapped some fish curry on the rice. He had caught the fish all by himself in the lily pond. When he brought it home, his mother could not believe it was he who had caught it! His father had taught him to cut the bait, line the hook, clean the fish, and he had become an expert at it all. But Appa was no longer there. One morning when Pakkiri was leaving for school, they brought Appa's body in a cart and laid it in front of the house. When his father was returning home the previous night after speaking at a meeting, some people had waylaid him and cut him up. There were more than a dozen slashes on his body which had been covered with a piece of cloth after the medical examination. Amma fell to the ground and wailed until some people carried her into the house. In a few minutes a crowd had gathered in front of his house and soon the police arrived in a jeep. The crowd became quiet. In the evening several people came from town and draped a red flag over Appa's body. One of them held Pakkiri's hand in a firm grip as the body was carried away, and Pakkiri followed behind in measured steps.

'More fish?' his mother asked, ready with another helping. 'No,' he said, 'I've already had four.' He jumped up, ran to the backyard, washed his hand and dried it with an old towel lying under the tree. Two mynahs flew down from the tree, and as he picked up a stone to throw at them, he heard his mother calling out to him. He dropped the stone, went to the door, and found his mother standing outside, carrying a small bag.

'Go to the loft, get the lock, close the house and let's get going. It's already getting dark.' She picked up a cloth-bundle lying under a tree, tucked it under her arm and began walking. Pakkiri locked the house, put the key in his pocket and hopped playfully behind his mother who had already crossed the canal.

The rippling waters of the river made a bend here. It did not seem as full as it used to be. He walked behind his mother along the bank of the river. A kingfisher was perched on a pungai tree on the opposite bank, its eyes fixed on the water. Any minute now it was likely to pick a fish. As he took another step, the bird swooped down and came up with a small fish in its beak. What fish was it? As he lagged behind, his mother shouted out to him, and he ran again, holding up his shirt-front. She chided him gently, 'If you dawdle like this, looking at everything, we will never reach our town. Come along.' Laughing, he began to walk fast, really fast, till he was almost running and his mother could not keep pace with him.

He stopped under a tamarind tree and turned around. His mother was quite a distance behind him, so he ran back, took the bundle from her, placed it on his head, and began walking beside her. She stretched her aching arm.

'Amma, are we going straight to our town?'

She looked up at the sky and said, 'It's pretty dark already. We will have to spend the night in Kadaramkondan.' Whenever they started for their town in the late afternoon, they usually spent the night in Kadaramkondan in his uncle's house, and set out again in the morning. He had stayed there several times.

The village was a short way from the river, and to get there they had to go through a mango-grove infested with jackals.

A group of monkeys — maybe ten or twelve — sat chattering under a banyan tree. He picked up a stone, and the leader of the pack came snarling at him. He hit it on the face and it ran away screaming, followed by the other monkeys. His mother scolded him, telling him it was a mad thing to do. Pakkiri walked on silently. The distance to the village seemed farther and farther as he got tired.

The river narrowed here a bit. It was dark now. The wind whistled through the bamboo trees. He waited for his mother, who took his hand and walked slowly behind him. They stepped down from the bank of the river on to level ground and walked through bamboo bushes and iluppai trees. They could now see the lights of the village. Mother and son went past the village and walked through another mango-grove. The dried leaves rustled under their feet.

'Are you frightened?' she asked.

'No,' replied Pakkiri.

And then, 'Amma, they are giving scholarships for the best students of the year. Teacher said I may get one too.'

'Oh, that's wonderful.'

'And if I continue to do well, they'll give me a scholarship to go to college also.'

'Oh! You must do your best!'

They came out of the mango-grove and crossed the canal. A dog barked. Pakkiri turned to look at his mother but her face was barely visible in the darkness. 'Don't get scared,' she said, 'It's nothing.' The dog stopped barking. They walked by the side of the tank and reached his uncle's house. Surprisingly, the house seemed locked. There was no sign of life on that street of ten or twelve houses either.

Amma hesitated for a moment, but catching sight of a lamp-glow inside, she called out, 'Anjalai!'

A silence greeted her, and she called out again.

This time a voice answered, 'Who is it?'

'It's me, Anjalai, Naagu from Injithoppu.'

After a while, the door slowly opened, and Anjalai asked them to come in quickly. She bolted the door as soon as they were inside.

Amma asked with a laugh, 'Have you and my brother been fighting?'

'No, Akka, don't you know there's been a murder in Kadaramkon-dan?'

'Who was murdered?'Amma asked as she sat on the floor. Pakkiri put the bag down.

'One of our people, I think. The police came and took away your brother this morning. They are looking for eight others, they are looking for them everywhere.' There was fear on her face and panic in her voice.

'Don't be afraid, Anjalai,' Amma said.

'But I'm so frightened, Akka.'

She lowered the lantern from its perch and said to Pakkiri, 'Will you have something to eat?'

Amma said they had eaten just before they left. There was a soft knock on the door. Pakkiri stood up and looked at Anjalai. She nodded her head, and he opened the door.

A group of women walked in, some with children at their waist, others clinging to their sarees.

'Anjalai, we are afraid to stay in our houses.'

Anjalai stretched out a mat on the floor, and the children huddled together on it. She lowered the lamp, and soon the feeble light made the darkness darker still.

Amma sat leaning against the wall, looking at everything around her. Pakkiri sat hugging himself. He stood up only when there was a knock on the door again. One of the children cried in its sleep. Asking Pakkiri to stay put, Anjalai cautiously opened the door. Three more women came in, and Anjalai bolted the door again. All of them sat in silence, overwhelmed by fear and grief.

The long night wore on. The women stretched out on the floor. The little children cried in their sleep. The lamp flickered and died when the oil was used up.

Pakkiri moved close to his mother, laid his head on her lap, and went to sleep.

Suddenly there was a commotion. The women and children were wailing, and Pakkiri woke up.

It was bright above, and when he looked up, he saw the roof was on fire. Sparks fell on them. His mother dragged him by the hand and rushed to the door, but she could not open it. She looked around, panic-stricken, but there was no way to get out.

A bamboo rafter from the roof fell down. The fire began to spread. People swarmed in that small room, trying to avoid the flames. Pakkiri looked around. The fire was moving from east to west. He rushed forward brushing aside his mother who tried to stop him. He jumped onto one of the walls and clutched a rafter, hoping to get out and open the door. But the entire roof caved in. His mother yelled, the women and children wailed, and the flaming roof enveloped everything. Then, all the noises faded, slowly, till they merged with the dying embers of the fire.

A police jeep arrived the next morning and stopped in front of the burnt house. An inspector jumped out and broke the lock on the front door. He came out a few minutes later and the other policemen trooped in. They brought out the charred bodies, and laid them in the shadow of the pungai tree. A lone vulture, circling in the sky, swooped down.

Translated by S.Krishnan

HOW DO WE STOP THIS?

THOPIL MOHAMED MEERAN

Malukku Muhammad lay prone on a reed mat, his head on a pillow, surrounded by his kinsfolk. All eyes were on his face. Some felt his hands, others his feet. Still others watched his nose to see if the breathing was regular.

The breathing was regular.

His eldest daughter sat by his head, intoning in a soft, fervent voice the *Yakuthba,* an Arabic hymn her father had loved. Behind that whispering chant roared and swelled an ocean of anxiety. With a full heart she sang for the spiritual peace of the father who was soon to leave her.

He had been in this state for several days. The *Yakuthba* and another Arabic hymn, the *Poortha,* had been chanted over and over again. Chanting such pious verses at a person's deathbed assured one a place in the company of angels in the hereafter. That was the belief.

'The pulse has weakened. At the most it's a matter of another twenty-four hours,' Doctor Murali had said, relinquishing the dying man's wrist.

They had brought him home from the hospital in a taxi, deciding that he might as well live out the last minutes of his life in the house he had built for himself. Three-quarters of that life had been spent in foreign parts. Mindful that death stood waiting at a distance of a few hours, they laid him down near a water channel in the courtyard so that it would be convenient to wash the corpse he was soon to become. Then they sent telegrams to all those who would want to see Malukku Muhammad in the little time he had left to live.

From distant places — homes from which they hardly ever stirred out — they came hurrying, men and women, to have a look at life finally removing itself from that body in which it had run and walked for some eighty years. His children and grandchildren wailed open-mouthed at the sight of the old man, laid out for his journey from this sin-ridden world to the other, sinless one.

There Malukku Muhammad lay, stretched flat; his dim eyes seemed to search for his children who had gathered about him. They glimmered weakly, deep down in their sockets, those eyes of his, bringing forth copious tears from the eyes of his family. Their cheeks wrinkled and formed deep canals for the gushing torrents of their grief. 'Vaappa!' they wailed, putting their lips to his ears.

'He can hear you, child! Don't weep, say the *Kalima* in his ear,' advised some people.

'Child, this is not the moment to dissolve in grief! Death comes to everyone. Pray devoutly for him, chant the Koran at the head of his bed!' entreated others.

From time to time everyone's gaze travelled to the wall that was not whitewashed; where the clock quietly chewed the cud of time, its needles moving like a tongue in its mouth. When they went past just one more of the numbers inscribed on that round face, it would be the hour foretold by Doctor Murali. What was now being stared at would no longer be Malukku Muhammad, but a corpse!

Now all eyes fixed themselves keenly on the clock's moving hands which had got past the hours, and now had to cross the minutes and the seconds. Once that was done, Doctor Murali's prophecy would come true, and the moment of grief would be at hand. With a silent footstep Israeel would enter, extend his invisible arms toward Malukku, pluck out his life, and vanish on the wings of emptiness.

When the minute for Israeel's footfall approached — that footfall which no human ear could hear — all the eyes that were rivetted on the clock-face turned to Malukku Muhammad's face, overgrown with white stubble. At the sight of those lightless, red-streaked eyes actually moving in their yawning sockets, amazement sprouted like new grass among his relatives.

The breathing too was normal.

At the last obstacle mentioned by Doctor Murali — that very last minute he had allowed for — Malukku Muhammad's life leapt over that sand dune of time like a horse that triumphs over its own sacrifice. His family stood around, shocked and uncomprehending.

And where was that Israeel, that soul of Malukku? Ashamed and cowering in the banana grove? To enter a house in broad daylight, and under the very gaze of his beloved progeny to open Malukku's rib-cage and to suck out his quivering life — maybe Israeel didn't think that was correct, and was hiding somewhere around the house.

Doctor Murali's calculations had never gone wrong. Until now, they had never heard of any patient whose hand he had dropped back on the bed ever surviving. Doctor Murali was eminently capable, an expert in reading the pulse. Though his deadlines were generous and allowed his patients plenty of time, they died hours, days, months earlier than they had to.

In Malukku Muhammad's case there seemed to be some confusion, but everyone felt that it was no reflection on Doctor Murali's computation. There could be no room for doubt on that score. More likely it was Malukku's pulse that was at fault.

They looked at the clock on the wall. As always, its tongue moved back and forth, saying its usual tick . . . tick . . . tick.

'Could there be something wrong with the clock?'

'Who says so? It was wound at the noon-prayer. When was that?'

'Half-past twelve . . .'

'Then why do you say the clock's at fault?'

'In any case, let's wait out the night,' an elder said.

Someone rubbed Malukku's lips with a little finger dipped in honey. One of the sons was wiping away the phlegm oozing from the corner of his mouth with a white cloth.

'It's a good death all right . . . with all the children around . . .'

'Not everyone can die like this, can they? Have you ever heard of a death like this one?'

The clock's fingers moved over the numbers in the usual way, at the usual speed.

The cavernous mouths from which sobs had escaped now closed up, and in the eyepools the tears froze. Late into that night they kept awake, leaving the door open for the angel Israeel to put in an appearance. But that heavenly being who leaned on a staff knotted with a silver thread did not arrive. Everyone felt irritated with him for having lost his way in the dark.

It would have been so easy for Israeel to come at the auspicious hour, with all the kinsfolk present! Noiselessly he could have reached out and opened the cage, and with his carefully-grown long fingernails pinched and plucked out the Ruh, the little chick of life. Their weary waiting could so easily have been avoided! As the burden of sleep grew heavier, yawns rolled out like railway tracks, long and endless. Some lit beedis, some lit cigarettes, others took a pinch of snuff. Yet others reached for paan . . .

Malukku Muhammad lay exactly as before. He could not move his body. Consciousness had not returned. From the regular breathing and the movement of the eyes they knew that life lingered on. From the rise and fall of the chest they were aware of the heartbeat.

Disappointed that Malukku Muhammad's death had not taken place on schedule, the neighbours scattered and returned to their houses. Some of the relatives lay down with their heads on their arms and went to sleep.

Those who awoke at intervals came to Malukku Muhammad's side and examined him closely.

'Has he died?'

'Hasn't he died yet?'

As time went by, they felt a new grief — that he had not yet died — and some of them felt terribly cheated.

Malukku Muhammad's first son-in-law climbed on to the coffin, patted it and examined it closely. It was made of first-class teak, and it was big enough to keep twenty-five sacks of paddy snug and safe. Only by removing the planks one by one could anyone take it apart and carry it away.

The second daughter's husband lay down, leaning against an almirah made of rosewood. How black and firm it was, he marvelled, stroking it. Its hardness made him despise modern steel cupboards. The rosewood almirah had been fashioned out of a single tree, back in the days when Malukku Muhammad had traded in forest produce. The son-in-law imagined it in the front-room of his house in Madurai. All those who set eyes on it would covet it. Those who had only seen steel sheets painted over to simulate the rich colour of rosewood would be wonder-struck at the real thing.

Again and again they looked at the clock, and turned away disap-pointed. Its thin fingers crept slowly over the numbers on the dial. Malukku Muhammad's life had not snapped and fallen off when Doctor Murali said it would. In fact, several hours had passed since that fateful moment when Malukku Muhammad's horse had begun its victorious journey. Perhaps Malukku Muhammad's death-spirit was hiding in the bushes, its eardrums bursting with the clink of the harness worn by Malukku's horse of life! Or maybe it was searching for those crushed on the highway, the victims of colliding buses. Possibly the details of his birth and life had not been correctly noted in the family diary.

Why hadn't Malukku Muhammad died yet? Hanging about them was this sharp sickle of a question mark. On the bumpy road marked off by the milestones of its numbers, that foreign devil of a clock was dragging along whole hours, and whole days too. Like a black curtain, sorrow darkly draped itself over the faces of Malukku Muhammad's sons, as the usual time for the Doordarshan broadcasts slipped by . . . the Sunday Tamil film, the cinema snippets, cricket, Oliyum Oḷiyum*. . . All these important things had to slink out of the way because an eighty-year old codger was taking his time to die.

Oliyum Oḷiyum (light and sound): a popular TV show featuring songs from Tamil films

What was the use of his living any more?

What was he anyway but a few bones twisted into a bundle of skin? Inside that skin, between the bones, a tiny tremble, that's all it was. If only that bundle, that clump of pubic hair, could have been stilled at last, they could have caught their buses and got home in good time!

As he lay asleep in Malukku Muhammad's own bed, his son muttered in his dreams of his not-yet-dead father. The bed was made of planks of wood from the jackfruit tree, set like gems in a framework of fine poovarasu wood. How pleasant it was to roll about on that smooth cot! It was not like the uncomfortably warm, cushioned mattress atop his own plywood cot at home. If this beautifully hand-carved bed were in the guest room of his house in a high-class neighbourhood of Nagercoil, all his guests would gape with wonder. The wood had a fine scent to it; that went without saying, since it was the best seasoned timber.

Night and day came and went, but Israeel did not come in search of Malukku Muhammad. The grave-digger came twice a day to make enquiries.

'Shouldn't I dig the pit, son?'

'No, not yet, please wait a little.'

'Is anything happening?'

'Nothing . . .'

The shroud-maker had made so many trips that the soles of his feet were wearing out. 'How many times I've come!' he said, rubbing his feet.

'Hold on a little longer . . .'

'It's only because I heard it was your father that I come here every day to ask. Otherwise it would be you who'd be walking all the way in search of us!'

'It'll be today or tomorrow,' the son consoled him and sent him away.

Defying everyone's calculations, the horse was galloping ahead over the seashore, kicking and stirring up the sand. And meanwhile, eighteen cubits of new white cloth, torn off and paid for, lay unused. Incense, attar, cotton to stop up the mouth and nostrils, camphor and rosewater

— everything was ready. All that remained was for life to depart. It would have to be buried at once. All else could wait.

They cut a mango-wood plank to size and propped it up against the stone wall of the big mosque. All the while, the wall-clock in Malukku Muhammad's house kept swinging the pendulum in its tail. Malukku Muhammad lay as before, breathing regularly, his eyes moving around, looking for who knows what?

Mucous trickled from the loose mouth. They spooned water between the rotten teeth. It did not go in but streamed out from both ends.

The *Yakuthba* and the *Poortha* resounded once again, sweet and melodious, from the throats of the women. The fragrance from the single red eye of the incense stick swirled and dissolved in the air. Like a smouldering fire, worry and grief — that death had not found their father — burned in the faces of Malukku Muhammad's children.

Losing patience, they stared often at their father's face, touched his nose with their fingers, and despaired at the faint warmth that emerged from the nostrils. The very lynchpin of their tolerance had come loose, but they did not acknowledge it to each other.

From the wall above, the clock's tongue voiced its tick . . . tick . . . tick. The sound blasted the ears of Malukku Muhammad's son and wrecked his peace of mind. As he glared at the tortoise-creep of the clock-hands, anger welled up in him. 'Tick . . . tick . . . tick' was the sound that kept awake the heartbeat, deep in the dying chest. To hold and stop that beating heart, Israeel had to come, Israeel who was Malukku himself! Where had he gone, without visiting this house? Why hadn't he come?

How many days had gone by as they waited? Wasn't there a limit to waiting, to their patience?

'Tick . . . tick . . . tick,' the clock's tongue continued to say, touching off a terrible rage in Malukku Muhammad's son.

He jumped off the cot of jack-wood planks set in its frame of poovarasu wood, and caught hold of the clock's dangling tongue as it swung from side to side. When it no longer moved, he turned around.

Near the water channel, on a reed mat, with his head on a pillow, lay
Malukku Muhammad, his chest rising and falling as before. The heart
within sounded louder than ever.

'Tick . . . tick . . . tick . . .'

How do we stop this?

Translated by Vasantha Surya

THE MIRROR

DILIP KUMAR

The tree, planted and looked after by the municipality, made that corner a very shady one.

Palaniammal bathed Jagadeeswari with a cake of washing soap and brought her to the shade. Jagadeeswari's head was clean-shaven. Palaniammal fetched a bundle from the box nearby, took out a tattered frock and dressed the child. The child, enjoying the gentle warmth of the morning sun, looked up at it and laughed.

Mariyappan, who lay curled around the tree-trunk in a semi-circle, woke up just then. Palaniammal looked at him as she tied up the bundle and put it back into the box. He sat up in silence. Palaniammal was very hungry. She had last eaten the morning before; nothing since then. Mariyappan pulled aside his torn sheet, and in an unhurried movement, fished out a beedi from his shirt-pocket and lit it.

As he drew in and exhaled the smoke, it occurred to him that he had no money for the next bundle of beedis. He had only one beedi left. But then he felt a mild courage grow in his heart. He remembered a twenty-five paise coin, stashed away in a knot in the corner of Palaniammal's sari since the night before.

The street had come alive. The child was watching the street with great interest and fascination. Palaniammal feared the inexorable moment when it would feel the pangs of hunger and cry out for food.

Mariyappan took a last, lingering puff of the beedi, flung it down and coughed. He gathered a big gob of spittle and phlegm in his mouth. He spat out the whole mess and stood up.

Palaniammal was staring into the distance, lost in herself.

Mariyappan washed his face clean and walked back to the tree, wiping himself dry with a corner of his filthy lungi. Palaniammal sat silent, her legs stretched out in front of her. The space around the tree, freshly swept, now appeared tidy. Two packing crates stood by the wall. Three mud-pots were stacked, one on top of the other, on one crate. The topmost plank of the other crate was missing. Several cloth-bundles, large and small, were squeezed into it. A black pot with a broken neck lay nearby. Beside it was a big tin drum, three-quarters full. The water in the drum was still. A small leaf, which had fallen from the tree, floated on the motionless surface of the water.

Mariyappan was very hungry. He came up to his wife and sat down beside her. When he began to speak, his manner was sly and ingratiating.

'Why don't you figure out a way for us to have some tea?'

'What can I figure out? Do it yourself.'

Mariyappan was silent for a few minutes. Then he began again.

'All right, leave it. But give me some money at least.'

'Where is the money to give you?'

'Just who are you trying to fool? Have you forgotten the twentyfive paise from last night?'

'Oh, that! That went a long time back. The child had tea in the morning. The remaining five paise went for a piece of tobacco.'

'Really?'

'Yes, really.'

Mariyappan grinned. 'No, you are ly . . . y . . . ying!' he sang out. He had a front tooth missing in his upper bridge. When she looked at her husband, Palaniammal felt pity and irritation. Then her hunger and irritation flared into anger.

'Yes! I'm ly . . . y . . . ying! Keep grinning like that all the time, like a toothless ape! Don't ever do anything worthwhile. Look at you. You call yourself a man! A man!'

Mariyappan had not expected this; his grin vanished abruptly. The next moment, he pounced on her like someone possessed; screaming crude abuse at her, he leapt and kicked her in the chest. 'Aiyo, Aiyo,' she cried out clutching her chest, tucking her head between her outstretched legs. His foot came down on her back. This time her scream was much louder than before. Perhaps it did something to him. With added fury, he crouched near her seated frame and gave her a hefty blow on the back. Palaniammal screamed again. He hit her again. She howled and cursed him. He punched her again and again like some maniac.

The child's mouth gaped with fear and she began to cry.

Mariyappan finally grew tired. His face streamed with sweat. He wiped his face and lit his last beedi. His eyes and forehead creased into a frown, he drew deep on his beedi and moved away from there.

The crowd which had gathered to watch this spectacle slowly began to melt away.

It was past two. The street baked silently in the sun. Palaniammal had fallen asleep, exhausted from the battering. Mariyappan was also sleeping some distance away. The child was awake, bewildered with fear and hunger.

A little later, the child grasped Palaniammal by the shoulder and shook her awake. Palaniammal was confused for a moment. Then she saw a girl standing before her. Although she immediately understood why she was there, Palaniammal loosened her long hair and shook it free. Then raising her hands to her head, she smoothed and patted down her hair, gathered it all tightly together and tied it back into a knot. The fair-complexioned brahmin girl, who had waited patiently all this while, asked, 'Amma, some brass vessels have to be coated with lead. Will you do it?' The girl was wearing dark glasses. She looked at Palaniammal's hair with longing.

'Mm, I will do it. How many vessels?'

'Maybe twenty, twenty five.'

'All right, just bring them here.'

'That would be difficult. You'll have to come and take them. There's no one to bring them here, you see.'

'Okay, where's your house?'

'Very close by. In the next street.'

'Okay, wait, I'll come with you.'

Palaniammal walked with the girl to the next street. The street was falling into an exhausted stupor. They barely spoke a word to each other. The girl walked at least a yard ahead of Palaniammal the whole way.

The girl's house was ordinary but huge; it was evidently the home of a large family. The girl directed Palaniammal to the pathway that skirted the house all the way to the backyard, while she entered through the front door.

Palaniammal started down the long alley. One of the rooms in the house faced this alley. A large cupboard with a mirror set in it could be seen through its open door. As Palaniammal walked past it, her reflection appeared in the mirror. She stopped abruptly and gazed at herself. She had never seen a full-length image of herself before. Palaniammal was startled. The form she saw appeared thin and tired. The mole under its left eye made it even more grotesque. The eyes seemed to be searching for something all the time. Time had not only devoured the body mercilessly, it had also robbed the mind inside of its youth. In that instant, she felt her entire life shrink before her, and then stretch out. The silence of that moment, empty of all thought, tormented her. Yet she found herself absorbed in that silence.

Then a few moments later, she moved away. The girl was waiting for her at the end of the alley. She was not wearing her dark glasses now.

Soon Palaniammal was back at her tree, carrying the vessels on her head. She had negotiated her fee with the girl and had collected an advance of two rupees.

She bought the child two buns and a cup of tea from the tea-stall across the street. Then she bought herself a cup of tea and drank it, and followed it up with a round of betel and nuts, and a little tobacco. She remembered to buy Mariyappan a bundle of beedis. After sending the child to buy rice from Nadar Provisions, she began her work with energy.

She dug a pit in the usual place, packed it with charcoal and lit the fire. Then she fetched from the packing crate the metal tube used as a blower, along with a small block of lead paste and a pair of tongs. She asked the child, who had returned by now, to stoke the fire. Then she began washing the vessels one by one. Mariyappan was sleeping like a baby. As she stared at him, she felt her anger begin to subside.

It was four when Mariyappan woke up. The fire had caught and red sparks flew from the cinders. Palaniammal was wiping the vessels dry. Mariyappan cast an eye around once and took in what was going on. Then he rose, washed his face and and sat down beside the fire. He picked a large pan from the pile of clean, dry vessels and placed it on the fire. Rotating the pan over the flames till it was uniformly heated all over, he touched a small rag to the lead paste and rubbed it evenly along the inner surface of the pan. The pungent smell of the hot lead and its vapour pervaded the air.

Palaniammal moved the beedi bundle towards him. Averting his face because he was too ashamed to look directly at her, he drew a beedi from the bundle and lit it. 'Hey Jagadeesu, go and buy a cup of tea for your father from the stall!' she ordered the child. The child skipped away happily. They worked till around seven in the evening and got all the vessels done without saying anything to each other. After tidying the place, Palaniammal placed a pot of rice on the fire which was still burning. Then she rolled a corner of her sari and made a cushion of it on her head, preparing to load the vessels. Mariyappan rose and helped her organize all the vessels on her head. Spitting out the betel leaf she was chewing on, she started on her way.

When she returned, Mariyappan was playing with the child.

Then at the usual hour, water began to flow from the municipal tap, and Mariyappan went to have a bath. Palaniammal went along to scrub his back. It was covered with layers of dirt. As she scrubbed, his lower ribs poked her palms. Pity welled up within her. After she had had her bath, she called out, 'Jagadeesu! Sit down with your father to eat,' inviting her husband obliquely. When the three of them sat down to eat, only the child ate eagerly.

It was ten at night when she was done with washing the dirty vessels. The child had dropped off to sleep. Palaniammal prepared to lie down for the night, tidying the space around the tree and sprinkling water generously on the dusty ground. The heat which lay secretly buried in the ground sucked in the water eagerly. Then suddenly the heat rose in the air, and the air slowly turned cool. As she did every night, Palaniammal hung up a sari that was not yet badly torn to make a private space for themselves around the tree. She laid the child on the worn coir-mat and spread another sari on the ground. Then, using one of the cloth bundles as a pillow, she lay down on her side.

Mariyappan, who sat leaning against the wall, flung his beedi away and moved closer to Palaniammal. She lay with her back to him. After a while, Mariyappan began, 'Are you angry with me?'

'Mm . . . hm.'

'Then . . . ? Sleepy?'

'Mm . . . hm.'

'Then?'

Palaniammal refused to speak. Mariyappan gently caressed her hands. Then he took her in his arms, turned her gently to face him and kissed her on the lips.

Palaniammal lay completely still. She was thinking of the full-length reflection which had appeared in the mirror. Suddenly she remembered that when she went back to the house to return the vessels, the room with the mirror had been shut.

She moved away and lay by herself.

Translated by N. Kalyan Raman

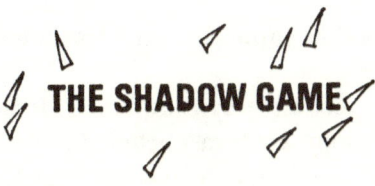

THE SHADOW GAME

KONANGI

'**G**reenie,' they called Koppamma of the Fifth, because she always wore a green skirt, not the usual blue uniform. And as if that wasn't enough, the teacher kept nagging, 'Don't bring your baby brother to class!' She would patiently reply every time, 'If I don't bring him with me, saar, my father won't let me come to school!'

After school Koppamma had many tasks. The laundry had to be fetched. Going from house to house collecting dirty clothes, and piling them in bundles on the backs of the donkeys, was something she had got used to doing a long time ago. It wasn't easy. The donkeys wouldn't stop meekly in front of the house for her to load the laundry. Each would wander off in a different direction. She had to get them all home.

The littlest donkey would never stand still. It would run to the top of the hill and look down at her with its small face. It wouldn't come close, though she called it 'Little Calf' and petted it coaxing, 'Your amma's home already, don't stand there in the damp!'

Kopamma walked up to it and stood a little way off, gazing at the tiny face abrim with beauty. It dashed away suddenly as she gave chase, leaping ahead of her yearning hands. How wonderful the donkeys in the dhobi colony were! Each was a marvel of beauty.

Her mother was proud that her girl went to school. But Chinna Thambi would start wailing the minute he saw her get ready to leave. There was no getting around it, she had to take him along, clinging to her like a baby monkey. He was spoilt, the last child of her parents. His bottom stank terribly, and no one else would go near him. He often made a mess in school. The entire class would make awful faces and move away.

Fifth Teacher set great store by cleanliness. He would order her to wash out the whole room. He firmly believed that not only the school but the whole world would go to rack and ruin the day he stopped punishing Kopamma the 'Laundress.' Weeping with shame, Kopamma would clean up, painfully conscious of all their grimaces. But not everyone made a face at her. There was Mariappan, who did not call her a laundress like the others. His name for her was Laundry Bug, which somehow wasn't so bad. Besides, he had his own troubles. They called him Flathead because his head was compressed flat in the front as well as at the back. He pinched them back, braving the punishing knocks the teacher gave him on his flat head.

Mariappan always wore a purplish shirt to school; he had three of them, all too large. Kopamma saw them when she went to his house to collect the laundry. They had belonged to his woodcutter-father, who had worn them with an old leather belt. As long as his father was alive, Mariappan wore nothing over his trousers. Then his father went into the earth, leaving Mariappan the three purplish shirts, none of which was the right shade of blue for school. All day long, one after the other, they taunted him with 'Flathead' or 'Purple Flathead.' But no grown-up ever did anything about it.

Mariappan's faded trousers were like cycle tyres with patches sewn over the punctures. Because he always kept lumps of jaggery in his pockets, rats gnawed holes in them, sometimes even while he was wearing them. 'Hey, Mariappa! Don't nibble jaggery all day, your teeth will rot!' his mother kept telling him, and he would answer, as meek as you please, the clever fellow, 'I won't do it anymore, Amma!' At the back of his pants, his bottom showed through a hole. The fellows in his class often put their hands in this post-box.

His uncle, Ponnusami Tailor, saved up bright bits of cloth to sew patches on his pants and shirts — all post-boxes of different colours. He sewed him a small purse, free of cost. No one else in school had one, just Mariappan. It closed with a press-button, and Mariappan kept money in it — pieces of paper torn from the middle of his notebook, on which he had drawn rupee notes, cutting them out with a blade.

When he had the other children's attention, Mariappan opened one of his post-boxes and took out his little purse. Heads craned over him. 'Hey, let me have some, hey let me have some,' everyone begged, holding out eager hands. Proudly he handed out rupees to everyone. At such times his eyes positively shone with a sense of accomplishment. He stuck a pencil in his mouth and strutted around like a lord, smoking it. Laundry Bug Kopamma stood apart from them, Chinna Thambi on her hip, watching them all. When no one was looking, Mariappan gave her one of his rupee notes. She looked around quickly before taking it in her hand.

Fifth Teacher entered, holding up the edge of his dhoti with one hand and clutching his cane with the other. The children called the cane the teacher's favourite book. One look around the classroom and he knew what mischief was afoot. It was because he had a machine in his desk drawer which reported every prank and culprit.

As soon as he sat down, he dismissed all those who hadn't worn their school uniforms on Monday. They couldn't enforce the uniform rule more often than that. By midweek most of the teachers would have forgotten who hadn't worn blue on Monday, but not Fifth teacher. He threw them all out. Then Kesavaal Ramaswami squealed, 'Saar, saar, Mariappan hasn't any pants on!'

Cane in hand, the teacher grabbed Mariappan and held him close.

'Saar! I do have pants on!' protested Mariappan, 'they're under my shirt!'

He clutched his shirt-front with both hands, trembling at the thought of his patched-up pants being exposed. With his floppy shirt reaching below his knees, he looked like a Catholic priest. The law of the cane cracked down on him.

The teacher looked around for the next offender — Kopamma, dressed unacceptably in green. To her too the cane spoke a sharp sentence. The next moment both Flathead and Laundry Bug were out of the classroom.

Outside the school they walked past the houses closed against the noonday heat. From the street-corner ahead came the sound of a class in progress. As if to celebrate their freedom, the heat too seemed to relent a little. Chinna Thambi rode on Kopamma's hip. The three of them approached the play-school where the shadow game was on under the great neem tree. That was where First Teacher Gopalan was.

The children of the Fifth had all learned to play the shadow game once, but it was now behind them. Fifth Teacher only gave lessons in English, Tamil, maths and science. He was the foe of all play. And parents were his allies against all fun.

With Chinna Thambi astride her jutting little hip, Kopamma tried to join in the shadow game, but the children refused to let her play. She stood next to Gopalan Teacher and watched them. The baby pulled and played with his sister's tangled hair. He chuckled as his tiny, tender fingers wandered over her face.

Though the children of the First took Mariappan into the game, they snubbed Kopamma and her brother, acting as though they did not exist. Gopalan Teacher seemed to be busy examining the neem tree, trying to find out when it had bloomed, when the blossoms had scattered, when the small, bitter fruit had ripened, things like that . . .

The children of Metupatti had played with the neem for years. The neem never forgot any of them. It had known even those who had taught Gopalan Teacher the shadow game under its branches. It was older than those who were grandfathers now. But perhaps because it was so very old, the neem tree may have forgotten when it sprouted from the ground, or how the shadow game came to be.

The neem saw Kopamma standing there, with no one calling her to play, chewing on the drawstring of her green skirt. Gopalan Teacher let go of the neem branch for a second and looked at the frolicking children. Then his attention swung back to the branch . . . how many branches, leaves, how many flowers had blossomed yesterday, how many of them had fallen today, how many altogether? The questions piled on each other like the happy bodies tumbling together under the tree. The neem tree nodded benignly over the shadow game, making a criss-cross of light and shadow. As the sun inched along, the shadows of the leaves followed it like watching eyes. The shadow game moved too — in the opposite direction, away from the sunlight.

Growing thinner every year, Gopalan Teacher continued to teach children to love the shadow game. Who knew how old the neem was? The games that flourished in its shadows would one day vanish, and no one would see them go. Here, where Metupatti began at the far end of South Street, this long stretch of dust would be blown away by the passing wind. The street itself would disintegrate and become nothing but a rutted track . . .

Not even carts passed this way now. No footsteps were heard. The dhobi quarter had changed, the houses were not the same, the families had grown, shrunk, scattered.

Inside the desolate courtyard of one of the houses, Kopamma smouldered. Her schooldays had long fled into the past, and she no longer even walked on the side of the street where the schoolhouse stood. She veered off to the cart-path that led into the jungle to fetch home the grazing donkeys and bring back an armful of thornwood.

All day long, under the fierce sun which everyone shunned, Mariappan grazed the landlord's goats. He all but became a part of the scrub jungle. Leaning on his staff, motionless as a stone pillar, his ears filled with the sound of the goats' dry munching on the withered foliage.

One day she saw him bawling, clutching his staff, as the goats ran amuck in someone's yard. Toddy-tapper Naadaar's brew had rushed up his head to meet the sun beating down on it. With blood-red eyes standing out from their sockets, Mariappan bellowed and sang till the jungle couldn't hold the clamour. It sounded as if he and the wind were beating each other up. Later, as he lay senseless on the stony ground, she saw that his body was plastered with thick brown sores, eaten through by his own salty sweat.

The purple shirt often moved around in the sunlit jungle as she gathered thorns. One night when she came to his house to collect the usual fee of cooked rice for doing their laundry, she heard him call from the darkened doorway, 'Kopamma.' She went towards him. He put his hand into her pot of rice, drew out a palmful and tossed it into his mouth. 'It's good,' he said. 'Kopamma, one for you too!' and he held another palmful out to her. She took it, but dropped it back into the pot.

From that night she made no rounds to collect the fee of cooked rice. Or the laundry. Her mother took over these tasks. Kopamma stopped going out, even to graze the donkeys or fetch the wood. She would stand at the edge of the wide-brimmed well and watch Mariappan driving the goats around it, sullen-faced, without even turning around to look at her. When he had to pass close by her, he moved quickly and soundlessly, and disappeared into the jungle.

Now, when no one looked at her, when no one cared what became of her, they came to ask for Kopamma in marriage. People from somewhere to the south, far away. They were fussed over as important guests. By nightfall it was all decided.

The next day she waited for a long time near the well, pitcher in hand. But he never came. When she reached home, she caught sight of a purple shirt, sticking out of a bundle of dirty laundry in the doorway. It was frayed; a complete wreck. When no one was looking, she drew it out and took it inside.

All rags and tatters it was, this purple shirt, with holes and patches everywhere. Deep inside her, a warm glow suddenly ripened and burst into flame. Sobbing, she held the reeking, sweat-soaked purple shirt tightly against her breast. She pressed it tenderly to her face. The ball of fire inside her burned on, refusing to be quenched. Kopamma put the purple shirt into the yellow cloth bag, along with the saris she was taking away with her.

In the pitch-black space beyond the back door, the night insects hummed loudly, adding to the darkness.

Translated by Vasantha Surya

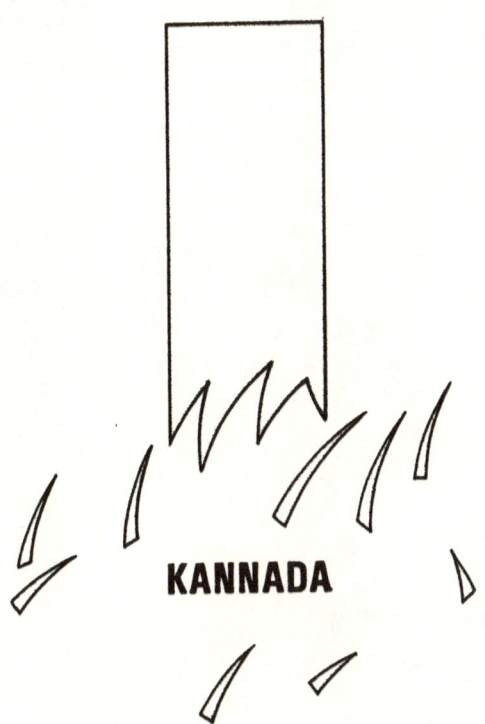

INTRODUCTION

To read fiction is to know the fate of a society through its metaphors. But quite often literature consciously takes upon itself the responsibility of exploring the state and fate of this society; this, I think, is what has happened with Kannada fiction since the mid-seventies. The two leftist literary movements of the day, Bandaya and Dalit, have contributed a great deal to this tendency. And that this mode of writing has grown from strength to strength is evident in the Kannada stories included in this volume. All the stories, except the one by Jayant Kaikini, are organically linked with contemporary issues and themes, and are deeply concerned with societal dimensions in presenting individual experience. In a sense, Kaikini's story reads like a metaphorical reaction to the dominant mode of writing today; thus his story too becomes an integral part of the Kannada literary psyche, although by default.

The stories 'Sahapathi' ('The Classmate') and 'Battha' ('The Paddy Harvest') examine concrete experiences, while 'Summaniralagadu' ('The Confession') deals with the region of the mind to understand a feminist theme in the context of the life of a middle-class woman. All four stories reflect the larger context of literary and philosophical ideas that have grown in the past two decades or so. Radical ideas and a search for alternatives have dominated the Kannada literary intelligentsia, and the Bandaya and Dalit literary movements are expressions of this milieu. It is an irony of our literary history that the four writers represented in this anthology, who have remained outside the institutional framework of these movements, have written more authentic stories revolving around these movements than the ideologues. Literature probably has its own way of ditching ideologues.

P. Lankesh's story, 'The Classmate,' interrogates with all the resources at its command one of the great temptations of our time: the

Gandhian ideal of the conversion of the heart. Like all great stories in Kannada, this one too has an appearance of being rough and uncut. The strategy is the compression of many decades of historical and ideological time into the apparently simple, realistic narrative.

'The Classmate' is basically a story about village India. Amid hatred and violence, the narrator tries to convert the landlord of a village. As a consequence, the story becomes a tale of the Great March to discover the fundamental truth about India. The narrative technique — the narrator's journey to meet his boyhood friend — invites comparison with another significant Kannada story, 'Suryana Kudure' ('The Stallion of the Sun') by U.R. Anantha Murthy. In Anantha Murthy's story, the narrator confronts the archetypal 'passivity' of Indian society. Till the very end, the story is Kiplingesque in its intellectual and emotional drama. But in the end everything is transformed, and the narrator gives up his suspicious and distrustful attitude toward the passive hero to identify himself with what he had earlier dismissed with contempt.

In 'The Classmate,' the narrator initially prescribes the Gandhian ideal of the conversion of the heart, without of course pontificating on its merit. But as the story progresses, the narrator confronts the basic evil of a society which has kept the caste system intact in rural India, either by force or consensus. He makes a journey, to suspend present-day categories for a moment, into the depths of evil in human beings. Eventually the narrator's belief system is destroyed in what is also a process of education for him. While the story essentially destroys the naive romanticism of a certain Gandhian vision of life, it validates, in a different way, the Gandhian understanding of the Indian village. Gandhi spoke about the village that never was. His idealistic followers mistook the utopian for the real. Gandhi, a shrewd and complex thinker, had tremendous difficulties with the real Indian village. Both the narrators of 'The Classmate' and 'The Stallion of the Sun' undergo an identical process, but radically divergent perceptions about the fundamentals of Indian life inform the resolution of the two stories. In Anantha Murthy's story, the narrator is animated by the sublime vision of the 'good' that exists behind the once-detested passivity of the hero. In Lankesh's story, it is the vision of evil that sends a chill of terror down the spine; yet the story does not scream. I would consider 'The Classmate' one of the most important stories in Kannada for its unconscious but ambitious efforts to wriggle out of the fictional state to face squarely the major questions of our age. In such a context, fiction is no mere idler's tale; it brings to literature a different kind of importance and dignity.

In the Kannada context, Mogalli Ganesh's story, 'The Paddy Harvest,' would be described as a dalit story. The village we have seen in 'The Classmate' is recreated here from a different viewpoint, with its full quota of caste wars between dalits and upper castes. In its generous moments Marxism has conceded these as primary forms of class struggle.

In the stories by Anantha Murthy and Lankesh that I have discussed, it is the socialist individual who builds the story. In 'The Paddy Harvest' and other samples of Kannada dalit literature, the narrative voice is mostly the collective viewpoint of the most developed consciousness of the community. Ganesh's story touches on one of the most important issues of contemporary Karnataka — the tragedy of the common lands. Vacant lands in rural Karnataka, meant for the use of the entire village community, have been more or less occupied by the powerful landed gentry. The landless dalits are now justifiably claiming these lands, and the traditional village is almost dead or on the verge of disappearing.

After its experience of state-sponsored violence, the old village in 'The Paddy Harvest' can never be the same again. The beautiful little village, the favourite theme of romantics, is permanently damaged and destroyed. Is this a good thing? Yes, good for the dalits, seems to be the agony-filled answer of dalit literature. We will no longer hear harvest songs. Indeed, Ganesh's story does not have a single one of these songs.

To put it more crudely, 'The Paddy Harvest' explores the myth of dalit emancipation through the will of the state. The tehsildar, despite his good intentions, only brings more humiliation and violence to the lives of the dalits. Ganesh's story movingly captures the different energetic moods created by the official promises of the paddy harvest. The entire dalit community has come alive to reap the harvest although they are not legally entitled to it. The initial euphoria is eventually replaced by an all-pervading gloom; but there is a subtle redemption of the earlier optimistic mood: 'As time passed, people melted into their own shadows. Mayamma's grandson, unable to bear his hunger, began picking up the cooked paddy grains scattered around the stove . . . *He stuffed his little mouth with them. It seemed as if he could digest everything.*' (Emphasis mine.) Thus the story achieves a political resolution without resorting to any theoretical cliches.

Ganesh's story, full of action and larger episodes, can be compared with the fiction of another important writer in Kannada, Devanoor Mahadeva (incidentally a dalit), whose 'Odalala' ('The Depths of the Body') covers the same ground as 'The Paddy Harvest.' Ganesh tries to achieve a kind of magisterial strength by making a large contingent of policemen descend on village-life like a pack of wolves. The vandalism they let loose is unbearable, not only to the victims, but to the readers of the story. Mahadeva, on the other hand, concentrates on a frail yet wonderful old woman, Sakkava, and the police in this case only take away one of her roosters. The difference in the structures of these two stories points to the existence of multiple modes of creativity within the dalit movement, and surely this is one of its strengths.

'The Paddy Harvest' is also interesting for other reasons. It reveals the existence of many crucial paradoxes in Kannada dalit literature. Although the story refuses to entertain any naive hopes regarding the will of the state towards dalit emancipation, its narrative tone is enlivened by a strange kind of optimism. What is being denied at the level of treatment of fictional material is internalized in the narrative viewpoint. This optimistic tone of dalit literature in Kannada is often surprising, given its background. Can this be explained by the upward mobility of the newly-educated dalits informing the vision of these writings? It could be a combination of radical optimism and attitudes of the upwardly mobile.

What attracted me towards Vaidehi's story 'The Confession' is the internal drama enacted by the narrator. The locale of the story is a train journey, although no specific town or route is mentioned; leading the reader to conclude that the journey is really an inward one. From its very first sentence the story has the quality of a secret cult about it. The narrator, a married woman, has a tale to relate, and it appears to be the rule of the cult to pass on the story to someone else. The art of such story-telling is at the very heart of women's survival.

In 'The Confession,' Vaidehi departs from her usual mode of writing which celebrates thick and dense details of women's everyday lives; here, she explores the fundamentals of a woman's world. The dangers involved in such an enterprise make the writer lift the experience out of everyday reality to place it in a twilight region that oscillates between modern story and feminist myth.

Narmada, the narrator, meets a woman on this train journey. The woman has killed her own mother. It was an act of great love by the nameless woman, for she could not bear the separation from the mother forced on her by her husband. It is precisely this kind of self-targetting by women that has enabled the patriarchal world to survive. The nameless woman asks Narmada a daring question: 'Tell me! Who should I have killed? Myself? My husband? Or . . .?' Narmada, still deeply involved in her married life, is too petrified to grasp the implications of the question. On the other hand, the writer is reluctant to answer this question in a straightforward manner. The success of marriage in a patriarchal society may mean the unbearable dissolution of womanly bonds, in this case between mother and daughter. Men have an intense distrust of such bonds.

Not surprisingly, the story brings to the surface the motif of recognition. Narmada desperately struggles to recognize the woman. But any real recognition would only bring a frightening kind of freedom to Narmada, who is not yet prepared for the birth of a new woman. At such levels of fictional and philosophical intensity, the story's attempt to open the door to forbidden worlds must have become too hot for the writer to handle! To face this challenge, the writer brings in the fairy tale dimension. Narmada suddenly remembers, and connects the woman before her with a face from one of her childhood stories. The structure of a story within the story should have enriched Vaidehi's story in more

ways than one. Unfortunately, Narmada's childhood story is not deline-
ated in detail and it refuses to mesh with the rest. Here comes to light
the inbuilt limitations of the natural mode of story-telling so ably
practised by Vaidehi over the last decade.

Jayant Kaikini's story 'Dagadu Parabana Ashvamedha' ('Dagadu
Parab's Ashvamedha') offers a delightful flight into a thoroughly enjoyable world of comic material. But it is possible to detect hidden explosive
material underneath the harmless jokes and laughter.

Kaikini's story is about the freedom that a writer takes with his
material. At the centre of the story is a wedding; through this the writer
arrives at a critique of the institution of marriage in a tradition-bound
society. Parab, the bridegroom, is taken away from his wedding procession by a galloping horse, only to replay the role in a near-fantasy context.
A radical writer would have treated this as an act of rebellion against
arranged marriages with all its usual associations. For Kaikini, untram-
meled by the dictates of progressive rhetoric, the rebellion lies in the art
of making the near-fantasy real. Marriages of love, unchallenged by
society, have always been among the favourite utopias of radicals, and
Kaikini endorses this idea in his own apolitical way.

The locale of the story is Bombay, like all mega-cities devoid of myth,
but the writer carves a modern-day purana out of the faceless multitudes.
The anonymity of a big city, and the freedom that goes with it, are
creatively transformed into strategies of taking tradition for a literal ride.
As in old puranas or fairy tales, Parab, the hero, is helped by fate in the
form of a horse, and Gulama's love is crushed by the rules of a real society.
Thus the real and the fantastic merge together to create a wonderful
story, in a literary culture where wonder and imagination on a large scale
have become taboo.

I have attempted here to delineate the background against which these
four stories were written. In all the stories, the context has been
transformed into artistic text and sub-text. The rest is left to the reader.

D. R. Nagaraj

THE CLASSMATE

P. LANKESH

Salutations to Shri Bhagawan, the highly respected writer, from S. Dyamappa, the Village Accountant of Kirumallige Village.

We are all well here and I hope you too are keeping well. The reason for writing this letter to you, sir, is the serious illness of Shri Basavegowda, landlord and former patel of Kirumallige Village. Recently he has begun to lose his power of speech. He has expressed a great desire to meet you. He has talked about your being classmates and sitting on the same bench while you were in the Middle School in Anandapura. He has followed your progress as a writer with pride even though the two of you haven't met for forty years. He hopes you haven't forgotten the Honourable Basavegowda. Your visit to Kirumallige village will surely bring some comfort to him in his present state of great suffering.

Please reply to this letter and let me know when you will be coming here. I shall receive you at the railway station in Anandapura and take you to Kirumallige. The village is in the middle of a forest forty miles from Anandapura. However, there is a motorable road. Please reply.

Your Most Obedient Servant
Village Accountant
Village Kirumallige
Kirigeri Post
Shivamogga District

I blew off the dust that had gathered on the letter which I had received six or seven years ago. My present intention is to narrate the experiences that followed. I've often tried to do this but have failed, not knowing where to begin, and from whose angle I could look at the whole thing.

I replied to Dyamappa's letter immediately and informed him that I would be there the following Thursday. He must have danced with joy. He wrote back promptly, telling me that everything was fine and that Basavegowda's condition had deteriorated further.

I had decided to go to Kirumallige as the visit promised an unexpected experience. I couldn't visualise the face of the man who was supposed to have been my classmate. All I had was a vague memory of our having had a mad adventure together: we had tried, in vain, to reach Jog Falls by a path that ran through the forest. There must be very little in common now between Basavegowda and me. Usually, such a thought is enough to put me off even thinking about a visit. This time, however, it filled me with enthusiasm.

The experience of a reunion forty years after having been classmates together, has a way of depositing itself in memory as so many unconnected pictures. Trying to recount the whole thing in detail is sure to make it unnatural because the intention is to make a well-knit story. And so I'll narrate the whole thing through pictures that I'm able to recall.

Dyamappa was waiting for me at the station when I got to Anandapura on Thursday. He was a dark, garrulous man, and seemed to me a loyal disciple of Basavegowda, though he worked for the government. Not knowing how to express the thrill he felt on seeing me, he snatched my case and bag and suggested that I have some coffee. I was in no mood for coffee and was upset that I had let myself in for all this. I even considered going back though I knew it was impossible to escape from Dyamappa's clutches.

He began his monologue as soon as he started the car. Kirumallige and its three sister villages were in the hollow formed by four hills. Not a single eucalyptus tree there. No poachers to fell either teak or sandalwood and cart them away. He described in detail the lake, stream and other water resources of the place. It was curious that he had not brought up Basavegowda's name till now. I didn't bring it up either, as though it was a mysterious topic. My responses were confined to a mere Yes, Is that so? and a Why, mostly to egg him on. The trees on the way were reddish in the violent colour of the evening sky. A cool breeze was blowing, as if to dampen the heady mixture of green and red. As we went on, the road, through the trees that seemed to kiss the sky, was shrouded in darkness. Dyamappa, talking as loudly as before, was coming round to Basavegowda. I learnt that he and Basavegowda belonged to the same caste and that the latter was a man of principle.

'What can I say, sir, if you haven't personally known your classmate's regal ways? He is the king of the four villages, Kirumallige, Taradaru, Manavalli and Moorji, sir. Our people don't even know that the post of the patel has been abolished. I am a distant relative of his, and since I arrived as the village accountant, we haven't had a visit from the amildar or shekhdar or Sub-Inspector. Basavegowda isn't a man of many words. Just a nod is enough, it speaks volumes. There are seven hundred houses of byadas* and kurubas* in the four villages, ten of lingayats* and a hundred of harijans, sir. No festival is held unless Basavegowda supervises it. No man can address a meeting without Basavegowda being seen with him. Shall I tell you what happened once? A young fellow from Bangalore lost his way and found himself among our hills. He said he was a communist and began ranting about how tragic it was that there wasn't a single literate person in the villages. He also spoke lightly of Basavegowda. Only four or five people heard him say these terrible things. But the news spread somehow and he was hounded out of the place after being beaten up. What incensed them was not his views but the way he spoke of Basavegowda. Thank goodness, we haven't had such mongrels visiting us again. Some time ago we had another group of boys here. They called themselves environmentalists, I think. They got Basavegowda's permission before going round the place. They were pleased with what they saw. It's ironic that poachers struck soon after their visit. Till then, not even a thorn had been stolen from the forest. As a result, Basavegowda gave strict orders that no outsider should be allowed into the place.'

---

byadas: hunters by caste
kurubas: shepherds
lingayats: higher caste followers of the twelfth century Veerashaiva reformist leader Basavanna

I had gathered meanwhile that he was a kuruba. Dyamappa's chatter also made some other things clear to me. Basavegowda had used his hereditary rights and the presence of four hundred kuruba families to lord over the four villages in that area. They led contented lives, since he had kept them away from a desire for freedom. They had also been spared the conflicts that go with modernization.

'Shall I tell you what happened meanwhile? Basavegowda used to get his books through me whenever I went to Shivamogga, and he read your books a number of times.' This startled me. I worried about the influence my books could have had on my classmate in this god-forsaken place. I tried to dissuade Dyamappa from talking about my books and asked him about the number of temples in the villages. He warmed up to the topic and told me of the Mari festival in Moorji and the chariot festival in Taradaru. There was no problem anywhere, at any time. The holeyas* would beat the drums, offer a he-buffalo as sacrifice and sprinkle its blood all over the place. The lingayats would immerse themselves in their puja. I changed the topic once more and asked how many families owned land. He began listing the names of all the landlords. Luckily there weren't many. It was getting to be a pain, talking to Dyamappa.

'Dyamappa, would you keep quiet for a while,' I asked.

'You shouldn't call me Dyamappa, sir,' he said. 'Dyama will do. I am nobody in your presence.'

He was silent for a while. I was beginning to feel that I had been caught in an unusual net. I had thought I had authored some revolutionary books. My articles and books dealt with the terrible sin of untouchability, the smallness that results from casteism and the tragedy of unequal development among different sections of society. I had expounded on the suffering of our people caught in the grip of casteism and corruption. But now I found myself unable to visualize the effects of my innocuous books in the context of these forests.

'Tell me, Dyamappa, in your villages . . .' I started.

---

holeya: an untouchable caste whose traditional occupation was the disposal of animal carcasses

'Dyama will do, sir,' he stopped me with the alacrity of a dog that has shaken off its leash, and then waited for my question.

'How many schools do you have in your village?' I asked.

'That's the problem, sir,' he said. 'Things were fine during the days of Basavegowda's father. We didn't have a single school. We had nothing apart from the platform around the peepal tree, the temple, the Mari temple and the place for the local court, and there was no bother. It was the same for the first thirty years after Basavegowda took over. No school, nothing. Things began going wrong when Basavegowda took to reading those books. Till then he was considered a silent man, but then he began talking to others sometimes. Kirumallige got a school. Earlier, only the children from Gowda's family learnt reading and writing. Even that problem had disappeared since Basavegowda had no children. Now we had a school. With it a teacher. A good teacher. He was a good man too in the beginning. He got on fine with Gowda. His name is Shivappa, a holeya.

'Things got mixed up after that. Maybe I shouldn't be telling you all this. But I can't help blabbering, I'm such a chatterbox. Don't tell Gowda I told you all this. His heart is tender though he has a rough exterior, like a double-barreled gun. He is a man of few words but his word is law. He speaks only after he has thought hard about what he wants to say. People from every community went to him and said they didn't need a school. We don't need things like that, they said. Gowda had read all sorts of books, you see. He wouldn't listen to them and we had a school, and Shivappa with it. No one trusted him. Remember the smuggling of logs that began after the boys from the environment brigade visited? People said Shivappa was with the smugglers. Basavegowda would have nothing to do with such rumours. If he had believed them, that would have been the end of our troubles.

'Do you know what happened in Moorji? A meeting was organized without consulting Gowda. Usually the people wouldn't have put up with this, but this time they kept quiet. It was said that Shivappa was behind the meeting though he had nothing to do with it. And then there was the instance of a lingayat girl having an affair with a byada youth. Our Gowda went about as if he hadn't noticed anything. The whole affair ended with a murder. Never before had the news of a murder in the villages reached the outside world. But this time, the police arrived and took away some four or five suspects. Gowda was furious. He sent for me and asked, "What do you plan to do now?" What could I do? My job was to maintain the accounts of the landlords, about ten of them. It wouldn't have been possible for me to keep them under control. Again, people said Teacher Shivappa was behind the whole thing. Gowda didn't believe them though he sent for him. Shivappa didn't turn up. We had all taken him to be a good and docile sort. Gowda went to Shivappa's place. The fellow didn't even bother to answer Gowda's questions properly.

"What's this, Shivappa?" Gowda said. "People are saying all sorts of things."

"I know nothing," muttered Shivappa.

"I'm glad you know nothing. It's better not to get involved in such things."

"I shall consult you before I get involved. All right?"

Gowda's eyes betrayed nothing. People had gathered round by this time. Gowda wasn't looking for any trouble.

"Plug your arsehole, you fat bum," Doddeera shouted. He was distantly related to Gowda and one of his close associates.

"Ask your master to plug his," Shivappa countered.

'Gowda didn't open his mouth; he walked away. That was all that happened. Everyone in the four villages heard about the incident. Rumours spread like wild fire. Gowda's rule went on as ever . . . let me stop here.'

Dyamappa fell silent.

His voice had grown distinctly faint as we approached Kirumallige. Darkness had fallen over the tiny place which seemed to rest in the midst of trees. We saw lamps here and there. The village had retired for the night though it was only eight in the evening. I was apprehensive about the coming meeting with Basavegowda. The car stopped in front of a huge house and Dyamappa opened its door for me. 'Gowda is critically

ill,' he had said, but I found Gowda on the verandah of the house as if
he wanted to call Dyamappa's bluff. I looked at him in the lamp-light.
He wasn't smiling. There was no sign of rapture at my arrival. 'Come,'
was all he said and it was obvious he was a sick man.

I was meeting him after forty years. He walked slowly and was only
half-alive. Both of us had grown up and then shrunk, each in his own
environment. There was no electricity in the big house or in the village
either. Gowda had to sit down on the bed and rest after he had taken
four steps. He seemed happy that I had come. Dyamappa fetched
Gowda's wife from the kitchen and introduced me to her. An open-faced
lady, she expressed her pleasure at my arrival, smiled and went in. I had
a wash and then sat before Basavegowda. He was silent. I looked at the
gray hair and sunken eyes in an emaciated body. He took me inside and
showed me his library. All the books were in Kannada. I noticed the
works of all the progressive writers, protest literature. My books were
kept separately. I didn't draw him into a conversation as it might have
tired him. I looked through a few of the books. He had marked some
passages with green ink and folded the corners of the important pages.
The house was much larger than I had thought. Four or five spacious
rooms at the end of which was the backyard. There was some light there;
some workers near the cattle-shed; and I could hear sounds from the
kitchen on the other side. The lady of the house was obviously busy
cooking.

I knew something had happened, but I didn't want to ask Basavegowda about it. Dyamappa moved about briskly as if intent on creating
a festive air in honour of my visit. I went with him to the backyard but
there were people there. He led me to the store-room in the corner. He
knew what I was eager to know.

'Won't you tell me what happened when Doddeera went at Shivappa,' I asked.

'I will,' he said and picked up the thread of his narrative. 'My master
didn't say a word. He returned home to sit on the verandah. All the
kurubas in the four villages heard the news. It was night when they
arrived, and they brought torches with them. They beat up Shivappa,

stripped his wife and continued to beat them as they took them out in a procession. It was a cold-blooded affair; there was no shouting or anger. After torturing them in innumerable ways, they threw them on to the floor of their house. Nobody was prepared to heed Gowda's words. Nor was he in a condition to advise them. It went on half the night.

'They didn't allow Shivappa to run away. It was as if he was a prisoner. No outsider was allowed in. The funny thing is that on the fourth night, there was a fire in the big temple in Malavalli. The men from all the four villages tried to put it out. They failed and the temple was reduced to ashes by the morning. Again, the people thought Shivappa had something to do with it. The atmosphere of the whole place has become rotten. The people are furious. The forests are being levelled, the police now come often, adultery and theft are on the increase and someone or the other starts a fire in the temple. People are convinced that Shivappa is behind all this. We have lost our peace and Gowda goes about enraged and frustrated.'

We joined Basavegowda for dinner though he didn't eat anything. Dyamappa didn't say a word throughout the meal and Gowda's wife was also silent as she served it. Basavegowda sent Dyamappa to bed and took me into his bedroom. We sat facing each other. As I sat silent, he held my hand and lisped haltingly, 'I'm very happy to see you here . . . though I have been seeing you in your writing.' After a long pause, he asked, 'Do you know what is wrong with me?'

I looked at him, waiting for him to continue.

'I haven't slept for twenty days. I stay awake through the night . . . because of the dream. The minute I fall asleep, the dream begins. In it . . .' He released his hold on my hand and grew serious. Basavegowda was not the type easily given to fear or tears. But he was shaken by what was happening to him. 'In the dream thousands of black people tear off my clothes, tie me to a pillar, make me eat all sorts of filth and lash me again and again with a whip. They throw me to the ground later and kick me. They pull out my father from his grave and torture him . . . Tell me, what should I do?'

I too was shaken; I asked him to speak of the nightmare again. He added a few details as he retold it.

'They drag me from the first floor and tie me to the pillar; or else, it's from my study or the bathroom. Once someone kicked at the bathroom door. There they were, the next moment, coming down the chimney. I screamed and woke up in a fever. I couldn't talk about the nightmare to my wife. I didn't think it was right to take Dyamappa into confidence. Not one of them knows what's happening. But I had to confide in someone. I stood in the backyard at midnight and recalled the dream once. Thank heaven, no one heard me. I came in and began reading. I read your book, *The Tragedy of Casteism*, twice. I thought about what would have happened to me if I hadn't read any of these things. But I couldn't help going back to them. All I know is that the more I read, the more disturbed my mind was.'

'Try to sleep,' I said and went into my room. A village in the middle of a frightening forest and a friend who could go neither forward nor back. I thought of his family which had ruled the place for thousands of years. I could hear the wolves howl and the bandicoots run. I couldn't sleep and I was thinking about Basavegowda. From his uncertain hold over his tongue, it seemed as if he hadn't exchanged a word with anyone for several days. I was wondering how I could help him. All the four villages were contained in his womb. The people knew him and most of them were his ardent devotees. He seemed to breathe through them. Like his forefathers, he had ruled the place for thirty years and ensured that the village continued the tradition of a hundred years. Whether it was a wedding, a festival, pulling the chariot or the sacrifice of a he-buffalo, he had to be there, giving orders, and making sure they were obeyed. A heart with undivided loyalty and love . . .

Then there was a sudden thud and the house shuddered. I was jolted awake; I broke into a sweat. I got up to go have a look at Basavegowda. He was not sleeping — the light in his room was clearly visible under the closed door. As I went back to my room, a small fear rose in me. He might have rolled off the bed or a wolf might have fallen off a tree. The house may have been torched like the temple. I tried to go back to sleep, but I was held back by memories from my childhood. I remembered the crippled Ninga, a madiga* who always suffered from an upset stomach. He was a grown-up boy by the time I reached high school. His arms were unusually well-developed, and their bulging muscles were clearly visible while he worked on our footwear. Once he asked me if I would put in a word for him with the authorities so that he would get a teacher's job. I was furious at his impertinence. When I was a boy it never occurred to me that a man of his caste could have a job. I left him with a brief exclamation of disgust. I never saw him again. What if he appeared in my dream? I was afraid. But I was soon overcome by sleep.

Basavegowda looked exhausted the next morning. He stayed in bed, having instructed his wife and Dyamappa to look after my comfort. I knew he wasn't asleep. I left the house with Dyamappa after breakfast. I had to do something, it was my duty. As I went round with Dyamappa, I noticed that the village was much prettier than I had thought. I saw tiled houses and cow-sheds with sheet-covers, and a huge lake on the way out of the village. The trees on the other side of the lake — tumbe, areca and palm — looked tiny. There was no need to ask who owned the plantations.

As I stood looking, Dyamappa reminded me that I had to see Shivappa. We went to the area where the madigas lived. There were small thatched huts; no sign of cattle. We stopped at the biggest house. When Dyamappa remained silent, I cleared my throat and called out Shivappa's name.

'Who's that?' asked a slim-bodied youth as he came to the door.

'Bhagawan. I want to have a word with you,' I said.

He didn't say anything. I went in and sat on the mat spread out for me. Dyamappa stayed outside.

I didn't think Shivappa was a bad sort. Though he carried wounds on his arms and other parts of his body, he hadn't lost his smile. Nor had he lost his courage. He had heard of me. I didn't know what I could discuss with him; I thought any mention of Basavegowda's dream would be tantamount to a betrayal. So I questioned Shivappa about himself. He was from the Nanjanagudu area, the son of a clerk. He had struggled

---

madiga: an untouchable sub-caste

to be educated. His brother was now in a hostel in Bhadravati, studying for a degree. Shivappa seemed to be in two minds about offering me a cup of coffee. I felt too inhibited to ask for one. I could hear his wife groaning somewhere in the house. Their child, a girl, was playing hopscotch with another child.

'Do you know what is happening here, Shivappa?' I asked.

'Do you know what my father told me before he died, sir?' he asked. 'Don't ever get involved in the affairs of the village, he said. I have never been interested in these matters. You must know what has happened here. I know I was rather rude to Gowda. Do you know why? I'd had enough of his men. I've done nothing wrong apart from that.'

I was flabbergasted. I hadn't come to his house to arrive at any compromise. My only intention was to find out the truth. But it looked as if my ignorance was increasing as I learnt more and more facts. As I got up to leave, Shivappa asked me to listen to a song. I sat down again, and he sang, with seriousness, a song about a boy and a girl who had got lost, very much like 'Long Ago, Angelo.' I thanked him and got up.

Basavegowda seemed to be sinking rapidly. His wife sat in the corner and wailed. The verandah and backyard were filled with people who didn't know what the illness was. They only knew he was critically ill. It suddenly occurred to me that I should take him to Bangalore. When I mentioned it to him, he rejected the idea rightaway with a shake of his head. He had not gone beyond the four hills for many years. He got his books through Dyamappa. But I couldn't think of leaving him in his condition; a power from across a gap of forty years seemed to hold me prisoner. Besides, there was the obsession that is a part of every writer. It was also a challenge I had to accept.

As days passed, Gowda's condition continued to deteriorate. He seemed to melt away even as I watched him. I was sleeping less and less, morning, noon and night. My life seemed to have gone off its track. On a Sunday, I sent for Dyamappa and asked if I could get some whisky. Dyamappa was taken aback; it was clear that there was a change in his estimation of me. But I had decided not to care about what he thought ·

of me, and I insisted on having some. He said he would get it from Anandapura and left rightaway. I forced some money on him. By the time he returned it was night and I went to the lakeside with him. I snuffed out the lantern he carried and sat down to drink. After a couple of pegs I had summoned enough courage. I walked back to Gowda's room.

'You are in trouble, Gowda,' I said.

He said nothing. After a long pause he asked, 'What do you want me to do?'

'Both your body and your mind have to be purified. If you do what I say, some of the mire may be washed away . . .'

'Go on.'

The entire forest seemed to hiss, and lightning struck as if to pull down the sky that had suffered all day from an asthmatic attack. 'Here it is,' I said.

He sat up. I didn't know how to say what I had in mind. I got up all of a sudden and went out with the lantern. It was raining and the glass of the lantern shattered, plunging us in darkness. Still feeling confused I came in and went out again into the rain. I called Dyamappa and told him what I had in mind. He was thunderstruck; he said I shouldn't think of such a thing. I didn't want to give up and continued to explain things to that dunce. Finally he seemed to relent and said, 'Maybe we can arrange it in his room without anyone coming to know about it.'

He went out, thrusting a ten-rupee note into the pocket of his shorts. Soon he returned with a black youth of average build. He was a holeya. He didn't know what the whole thing was about. I sat with him in the cow-shed and told him what I wanted of him. He seemed to understand only part of what I said. Meanwhile, Dyamappa had gone in and got Basavegowda's consent for what was to follow.

The rain had eased a bit and I took Joni — that was the name of the boy — from the cow-shed to Gowda's room. He was alone and he stared at me as I went in. Everything was ready for the puja. Dyamappa had explained things to Gowda, who was hovering between life and death.

It was eleven in the night; the rainwater dripped from the trees in the backyard. Gowda sat up, while Joni was on his feet. As Gowda picked up the brass mug, I asked Joni to place both his feet on a silver plate. Gowda's hands trembled as he washed Joni's feet. It was obvious that my silence was a driving force, pushing Gowda into the act. His entire body shook, as if caught in an earthquake. He rushed through the ritual of washing, smearing vibhuti and scented water, tucking a flower in Joni's hair, and waving the platter with a burning lamp round his face. 'Your mind too should act like this . . .' I said.

I sent Joni home with some more money. Gowda sat down on the bed as if utterly spent. I spoke of psychology and sociology to prepare his mind. Also, of the complex nature of the unconscious. Gowda was dropping off. He tried to fight sleep but couldn't. Dyamappa took me to his room. He knew of Gowda's insomnia but had chosen not to tell me about it.

I didn't see either of them in the morning. But I was happy that Gowda was able to move about once again. There was no trace of them through the afternoon or evening either. Gowda's wife served me dinner, and it was around midnight that I saw them come in, just as I was beginning to get worried. They didn't answer my questions. I announced that I was leaving in the morning. 'Stay,' was all that Gowda said.

'Did you sleep well?' I asked.

He didn't bother to answer. He seemed to have changed. I didn't know where he had been for the day, but his face seemed to have got some of its colour back. Dyamappa was tired from all that loafing and he didn't say anything. If Gowda, who had turned into a living corpse with sleeplessness, had been out all day without even asking after me, he must have had a dreamless sleep, I thought.

'Tell me the truth. Did you sleep well?'

'No,' he said but I didn't believe him. I had watched him at dinner and seen him eat more than usual. Dyamappa too had cheered up. It seemed that Gowda had got back some of his freedom, and I thought I had achieved my purpose. I packed all my things but I began to feel that a great falsehood was devouring me and I took out the bottle of the night before. I called Dyamappa into my room and implored him to say something or the other.

There was a cool breeze, still moist with last night's rain. The events in Kirumallige had left me confounded. But how beautiful nature was, in spite of all the efforts of poachers, brewers of illicit liquor and arsonists! I poured a second drink which helped my mind soar above the meanness people are capable of. I called Dyamappa all sorts of names. I accused the son of a slut of having inveigled me into all this with his colourful words. I charged him with having wilfully kept many things from me.

It must have been several hours later that Gowda, who had been snoring, suddenly let out a blood-curdling scream. Dyamappa and I rushed to him. We asked him to open the door that was bolted from inside. His wife also pleaded with him. Minutes ticked away and we could hear him inside, sobbing. He finally opened the door and collapsed on his bed.

'Give me a drink,' he begged.

I told him I had decided to leave.

'Please don't,' he screamed, through grief-stricken sobs.

There is a certain cowardice, and a helplessness, in sobbing. But there was only grief in his sobs, the grief of a man close to death. I had decided to leave because I felt he had not confided in me completely. 'Save me,' he begged.

'The tale of a million years is hidden in the frightening darkness of man's mind. The roots of the institutions an individual builds, the events in his life which touch him, his vanity and inferiority, are all there in that darkness unless he is content with just eating, copulating, growing old and fading away when the time comes . . . Feelings like vengeance, guilt and challenge are inevitable for such an individual . . .' The words came out of my innermost depths. But though Gowda and Dyamappa were listening, it didn't look like they understood the significance of my words.

'Save me,' Gowda implored. I somehow thought he had said, 'Save my honour.' Though life and honour are one and the same thing, they seemed to be in conflict in his life.

I had another drink. I fished out the packet of cigarettes from my suitcase and began to chain-smoke. Gowda continued to moan through his sleep-cheated silence.

'I'll see that you don't ever dream again,' I said. He seemed to have faith in my promise; he sat quietly through the rest of the night, dozing every now and then.

'Do as I say today,' I said. He nodded like a child.

I sent for Dyamappa, Duruga, Basava, Taraga and others. They were his men, and I told them what they had to do. It was a clear morning when the men set out with their drums to call the people of Taradaru, Manavalli, Moorji and Kirumallige to a meeting that evening in front of the local temple of Choudeshwari. People gathered all round the platform that had been put up, curious about this summons from Basavegowda for whom they had respect mixed with awe, whatever their caste loyalties were. They were innocent people, far away from the divisions and tumult of the cities. I had told neither Gowda nor Dyama of my plans. As evening fell, my inner turmoil surpassed that of my friend.

I led him to the meeting, where four torches lit the four corners of the platform. Dyamappa had come with Shivappa, just as I had asked him to. I had asked Gowda's wife to bring whatever was necessary for a puja. She too had everything ready. I got on to the platform, asked everyone to be quiet, then described the mental agony Gowda had gone through. They didn't seem to understand anything though they had taken Gowda's illness to heart. 'May I request Honourable Shivappa to join me?' I said. I whispered in his ears. He didn't seem eager to do what I had in mind. 'Please say yes,' I pleaded. Basavegowda came up and I said to him gently, 'I want you to go through last night's ritual, here in public. It's Shivappa this time, not Joni.'

Gowda broke into a sweat. He looked helplessly at the people. 'You must do it if you want to save yourself from the nightmare,' I said.

As he washed Shivappa's feet, the people closed in and I felt their breath touching our bodies. Shivappa shook in embarrassment and fear.

Death seemed to be closing in on all of us. Basavegowda went through the motions of washing Shivappa's feet, smearing them with vibhuti and scented water, burning incense and putting a flower in Shivappa's hair, all in a stupor. His body shook uncontrollably. The people were furious as Basavegowda got up and folded his hands. He embraced Shivappa. He seemed to have been irrevocably caught in a mesh, and he had taken his people with him.

In a voice tinged with sleep, anger and regret, he whispered in my ear, 'Do you know where we were last night? We went to rape Joni's wife. Forgive me, friend.' He then lay down on the platform.

His words struck me like lightning.

I raised my voice and repeated what he had said to the people.

I had to do it. Otherwise the people, infuriated by the puja, would have set fire to the place. I spoke about his immoral act and his arrogance.

Even then I felt I had committed a treacherous act. What sort of treachery? Against whom? I didn't have time to think over such things though. I had to flee to save myself from the people.

People began to sit down; their primary concern seemed to be Gowda's health. Perhaps they were wondering how they could face him afterwards.

We had enough light from the four torches. Gowda seemed to be asleep, even snoring, as he lay stretched on the platform. I was wrong, there was no snoring. The silence of the people seemed to have merged with his own. As Shivappa got off the platform, I placed my hand on Gowda's body and found it cold.

He was gone.

People cried as darkness deepened. I was moved by their helplessness.

It is only now that I am able to put down on paper something which lay hidden in me over the years.

I was in a daze about the event for a whole year. I even began to have doubts that I had gone to Kirumallige at all. I have asked myself what would have happened if Basavegowda hadn't died that night. I have thought of the life of a leader full of sin, guilt and vengeance. I have even tried not to think about such things . . . Just as I was telling myself that

there's a message in what happened, there was a letter from Dyamappa.
It was written a year after the event.

Respectful salutations to Honourable Shri Bhagawan. We are all well
here. Please be good enough to let us know that you too are fine.

Chandramma, the wife of Basavegowda, died the other day. A distant
relative of his now lives in the house. Moorji also has a school now. A
bulldozer levelled the forest here in July and eucalyptus trees have been
planted in its place. There will be no more poachers as a result. Joni's
wife ran away with someone. We have been told that Kirumallige will
soon have a police station.

Your Admirer and Disciple,

S. Dyamappa

Translated by Ramachandra Sharma

DAGADU PARAB'S ASHVAMEDHA

JAYANT KAIKINI

The wedding procession had turned slowly towards the station from Lal Bahadur Shastri Road in Mulund, and proceeded down the main bazaar road. The band, like brocade-clad gurus, led the procession; behind them were teen-age boys with shiny moustaches. Next, middle-aged men in T-shirts that stretched tightly across their stomachs, preened themselves as they walked through the bazaar, glancing every now and then at their wives behind them. After them, a strange crowd, drunk and dancing, with red powder smeared all over. Right at the end, like the brake-van, came a group of women.

And in the midst of all this was the veiled bridegroom, sitting atop a light brown horse, as if he was a part of its vertebral column. The strands of jasmine suspended from his gold-laced turban covered his face. A feather was about to fall off the turban. No one in the procession could remember the face of the bridegroom, Dagadu Parab. The man walking like the President, a little ahead of the horse, to the right, was Balachandra Parab, the bridegroom's elder brother, the one who had planned the alluring spectacle of a horse in the wedding procession — personally persuading the bride's people — running around to fix up a horse and supervising the procession from home to the mantapa put up at the bride's house. So he walked now, watching his little brother on the horse or looking at the people in the bazaar. The fact that he was solely responsible for the first horse-procession in their lives was obvious from the way he looked around him.

The procession moved down Shivaji Road to the Shivaji statue. It was just about to go past the statue when a motorcycle in a garage nearby got kicked and screamed its guts out. The entire bazaar was stilled for a moment by the sudden sound that pierced the sky. And before anyone could blink, the horse lifted its forelegs and neighed; the bridegroom too yelled in a strange voice and swung this way and that, undecided which way to fall. The horse galloped away like lightning along with the bridegroom.

Following the speechless moment when all this took place, behold, a commotion erupted! The people in the procession surged into any street that caught their eye. As soon as he recovered from the calamity, Balachandra stuttered something to all of them and rushed into the vegetable market to the left. Here everybody was immersed in shopping bags, change and vegetables. They didn't seem to have noticed the horse galloping across. Balachandra Parab ran back to the statue as if something had suddenly struck him, and told the women and those left behind from the band to stay right there. The women moved to the side of the road because it was impossible to stand right in the middle. But they were driven back by a fruit-seller whose shop they had gathered around.

All this while, Balachandra's wife tittered along with the rest of them. She knew quite well that her husband had taken on this mammoth exercise out of pure spite, just to drive home the fact that her father had not engaged a horse at their wedding. So she laughed to herself and kept quiet.

Parab, however, was utterly confused. 'Dagadu . . . Dagadu . . .' he jabbered as he ran in and out of the vegetable market till he was at Goshala Road. The grim question before him was where to find the horse. If it was found, would Dagadu be on it still? Or should he look for Dagadu alone?

Meanwhile, the volunteers who had pushed their way into various streets looked only at the ditches on either side of the road. Perhaps Dagadu would be lying there. A school had been let off in Goshala Road, and the children were at the mercy of the traffic. Balachandra stopped them and asked, 'Did you see a horse running down this road?' Parab was disgusted when he had to ask the people waiting at the bus-stop ahead the same question.

At the same time, the whereabouts of Gulama, the fellow who had brought the horse, loomed up like another question before him. Balachandra told himself that he must have also gone looking for the horse. In any case, he should be more anxious about it than anyone else. Deciding to look only for his brother, Balachandra engaged a rickshaw and roamed about different roads and alleys. He stopped here and there. The baskets at a distance looked like horses. Dagadu seemed to be standing by the side of a road. Balachandra was bewildered; he stopped the rickshaw as soon as the metre registered sixteen rupees. Now he was far away from the suburbs, near a playground.

Gulama, the boy who had brought the horse, had disappeared in the midst of all this commotion. As soon as the horse neighed and took off, Gulama had run to the station and taken a train to V.T. The horse wasn't his. It belonged to Bhanumati's father — Bhanumati, whom he loved secretly, and who inspired in him a clandestine lust with which he struggled desperately.

Gulama worked in a grocer's shop in Kalava. As he was packing some groceries, he caught sight of the girl living in the stable-like house across the street. He fell for her arms rightaway. He watched the way she swung her arms, without lifting them to reveal her armpits, as she hung the clothes to dry. Gulama became a gulam.

Her father's sole business was horses. He was supposed to have been a tongawalla long ago. Now he had four or five tongas. He would send the horses and gaadis to Juhu Beach for children to ride on during the holiday season. In that house which was so like a stable, with nothing but tongas, horse-dung, horse-tails, horse-feed and horse-gram, Bhanumati had also noticed Gulama. She swelled up, smiled and disappeared, swan-like; she played with him using just her eyes.

One day — who knows what happened — Gulama went up to her father openly and asked for her hand. Her father offered his own hand instead; and with such sharpness that Gulama almost died of the insult. But since he had acquired, from Hindi films, an unshakable faith in the victory of true love, he didn't give up watching her white arms as he packed groceries. He shot her angry, stubborn glances of love. He made friends with the tongawallas. He even tried to provoke Bhanumati's attention by serving young female customers in a leisurely manner and flirting with them. One fine day, when this play-acting got out of hand, Bhanumati stopped looking at him altogether.

Then, not knowing whether he was fed up or angry, he began to while away time with the tongawallas in the bus stand at Thane. It was in the midst of such idle chatter that he heard Balachandra Parab haggling for a horse for his brother's wedding.

Gulama was suddenly filled with a strange bravado.

'Give me as much as you can afford. I shall bring the horse early in the morning,' he promised. 'But I can't be responsible for decorating it and all that.'

The next day he got up at the crack of dawn, untethered a horse from the stable belonging to Bhanumati's father, walked it all the way and presented himself at Parab's room in Mulund. Parab's neighbours came out in full force, eager to decorate the horse; but the horse's bad temper drove them back. Eventually, beautifying the horse was given up as impossible, and the decorated bridegroom was hoisted on to the horse with the help of a stool.

When he saw the horse, which seemed to have jumped out of a film poster right up to his door, Dagadu Parab was greatly agitated. He forgot that he was the bridegroom. He felt that his life would end if the horse merely shook its head. He had broken out into a sweat by the time the procession started. Why on earth was he born as a younger brother to this elder brother? As soon as the band struck its first notes, the horse jumped ever so lightly, and his backside was badly hurt. Dagadu shifted his bottom a little, trying to soothe the pain, when he was struck again at the very same spot. Now he lamented over the very fact of having been born a human being. Meanwhile Gulama walked on, impassive.

Gulama had wanted to get away as quickly as possible; but a wedding always means girls, wearing outsized blouses and coming up to the guests over and over again to smear attar on them. Gulama, an immediate victim of this attraction, stayed on with the procession. Balachandra Parab even got him a Gold Spot. Just as they neared the Shivaji statue, Gulama finished the drink and the horse escaped. He looked neither this way nor that as he ran to the station intending to go to a film. Safely seated in the train, he did not forget to curse Bhanumati and her father with total destruction.

When Bhanumati's father woke up at eight in the morning and discovered what had happened, he began jumping about with rage. He sent some of his tongas to the Kalava-Thane area just to look for the horse. He made a complaint at the police station. There they asked him what colour the horse was. 'It's the colour of a horse,' he said, not knowing what else to say. Bhanumati, however, was filled with some exuberant feeling all morning. She went to her bath, singing as she washed and scrubbed herself.

Meanwhile, someone narrowly escaped being beaten up when he asked Balachandra Parab, who was walking anxiously across the sunny playground, 'You? Here? It was your brother's wedding today . . .'

For a moment the wedding pandal, his township, and his tenement seemed far away. If the horse and Dagadu had not run away, the wedding would be taking place right now. Balachandra began to worry that they might have got back to the venue of the wedding, and that everyone would be looking for him. He considered going to the police station. But the thought of a license for the wedding mantapa, for the use of speakers, and all the usual payments to be made to the police made him feeble.

Dragging his feet, he reached the mantapa around two in the afternoon. Many people had waited there endlessly; some women had fallen asleep where they sat. The members of the band and those who had come to see to the speakers went in and out of the kitchen with toothy smiles.

Around three o'clock, Parab stood up suddenly. 'It's all God's will. What has to happen will happen,' he said, and ordered that lunch be served. The hungry gathering attacked the food. Parab absent-mindedly ate a jalebi his wife forced on him. But his heart was in his mouth when he had to pay the full amount to the band which had played only two songs. Yet he managed to count the notes as he handed them over, making sure there were people around him, watching. When the man with the speakers wanted to know if he had to stay till the evening, Parab shouted at him, 'Go if you want to.' Then he sat on a chair and nodded sleepily.

What happened to the horse near the Shivaji statue? That horse had been in a circus for a while. It had also taken part in a film-shooting for a few months. Its memories were far from ordinary. Who knew what memories of the circus were raked up in the horse's mind when the motorcycle stuttered? At that very moment it had jumped up, lifted its forelegs and galloped away. It had already been provoked by the unnecessarily involved affairs which had begun early that morning. The sudden noise was as much as it could take. Thudding along and jumping, it reached Rajaji Road, turned on to Jhaver Road, and ran towards Goshala Road.

On its back, Dagadu swung like a pendant. He had clutched the horse in such an embrace, and closed his eyes with such resolve to become one with the horse's frisking, that he forgot the miracle of not having fallen off yet. He began to neigh strangely. Children from the schools in Goshala Road crowded around and shouted 'Hey!' Even that didn't affect him. But his turban fell off there. Some of the children caught hold of it and raced behind the horse for a few minutes.

The horse turned and ran through the large playing fields of St. Pais, among cows and a few cricket pitches, jumped over a small wall, joined Agra Road, cantered through the small area by the petrol bunk, before it began to run amid large vehicles, trucks and double-deckers. People in buses watched Dagadu who had lost his turban. Now the horse began prancing about among the vehicles.

At that stage, Dagadu lost even the little active relationship he had with the workaday world and became one with the horse, experiencing a strange lightness. His job at the mill, his brother's bullying, the bride with buck-teeth, his useless daily activities — he seemed to kick them all firmly as he held on to the horse's neck. For a moment, he was Shivaji climbing Raigarh Fort. The horse was racing along the highway, past the octroi post, jumping signals, racing towards a destination only it knew.

It ran like this for quite some time, left the highway, went over familiar by-lanes, entered a suburb, panting, breathing hard, slipped into a very narrow alley, and stopped at the courtyard of a stable-like house. Some men came out of the house and brought Dagadu down, all worn out and hanging loosely to the reins. They undid his brocaded buttons, fanned him and laid him down on a charpoy. A girl with a pot full of water appeared, and stood before his floating eyes. As he gulped down the water noisily, she disappeared, singing softly to herself. Without too many words, within two minutes, Bhanumati's father accepted this ready-made bridegroom who had brought the horse back, as his son-in-law.

Many months later, someone brought the news to Balachandra Parab — Dagadu was giving children rides in his beautiful tonga in Juhu Beach. That very evening, Balachandra Parab took his wife and children, travelled by a train, and changed two buses to reach Juhu. What a sea of people, how many tonga-horses, camels, children, balloons were on the beach! But there was no sign of either Dagadu or the tonga carrying him. Balachandra wandered around till his legs ached. He bought his wife and children packets of chana and wandered off again before coming back tired.

Seeing his disappointment, his wife mumbled, 'Didn't you find him? If you had found Dagadu, we could have asked him to pay back at least what we spent on the mantapa and the wedding lunch.'

'For heaven's sake!' Balachandra burst out angrily. 'That was the least I could do as an elder brother,' he added, gazing at the sea mournfully.

Translated by Padma Ramachandra Sharma

THE PADDY HARVEST

MOGALLI GANESH

Muttanna's forge blazed like a small factory as the scythes fell in a heap around him. The rhythmic clinking of the hammer on the anvil, the hissing of hot metal suddenly dipped in cold water, the murmur of people, their breathing, coughs and laughter, and the snake-hiss of the furnace, all together created an incredible sense of life in the night-black colony. As the flames from the furnace rose, the shapes of those gathered there expanded and shrank by turn, as if they were waiting eternally, devoutly, for some joyous event. As Muttanna's sweaty body swayed, the crowd carefully gauged the sharpness of the scythes emerging from the furnace. Never before had Muttanna put the furnace to such use. He was sharpening every customer's scythe to a fine point, as he wove dreams of the vast quantities of grain all this work would fill his house with. The people of the colony usually paid him paddy, not cash, for tending their scythes.

The next morning, they arrived at a collective decision to harvest the crop in the paddy fields of the Olagere plain.

There had never been so much bustle and hope before in the history of the colony. Their dreams of gold-hued paddy, transformed into an illusory, alluring enchantress who filled their homes with wonder, grew moment by moment. The front-yards of those who did not need to hone their scythes afresh filled with the metallic sounds of tools being sharpened on stone slabs. The small children, eager to take part in the elders' activities, were trying hard to drive away their sleepiness. The women fondly ran their hands over dust-covered pots lying helter-skelter in corners; they boasted of their 'high-class' vessels that would be used to store tomorrow's paddy.

Some old scold muttered, 'I told the wretched fellows a thousand times — don't do it. Don't ruin these vessels, don't sell them. But who listens? They sold the mud pots to feed their bellies. And who should I go to now and beg for a vessel to collect tomorrow's paddy?'

Her anger had a history. Years ago, her ancestors used to steal cattle, slaughter them and eat them, not leaving a trace behind. They filled the storing vessels with the remaining bones. Then they dug pits in the backyard and buried them. This was how they escaped detection by the cattle-owners. This was how they hid the hunger of their bellies while saving their honour. Then the backyard was dug up for some reason, the vessels were removed and sold. The old woman was inconsolable; she saw this as the public sale of her family's honour. She felt not only sorrow but also rage. Now, remembering this bit of the past when it was time for the paddy harvest, she ranted against the members of her household.

That night, the stars in the sky's garden looked like paddy grain, hung for drying; or scattered for sowing. This encouraged them, and made them more determined about their plans for the next day.

The noises from the forge melted and merged into the old woman's loud cursing. People came out of every house and collected at one place, as the nymph called paddy danced in a myriad ways. One said, 'The last time we ate rice was during the last harvest.'

Another interrupted, 'No, no. Didn't we eat a sumptuous meal at the death anniversary of the headman's wife?'

A third cut in with enthusiasm, as if he had to blurt it out before it fled his memory forever, 'Good Lord, what are you talking about? It was the feast you ate in the house of Dase Gowda. How can I describe the glory of that meal, recount its magnificent story? There was rice palav . . . served on plantain leaves . . . and what a beautiful smell . . . The lovely aroma of spiced rice filled the room, so that the entire house seemed to be something made out of sandalwood. Well, I have enjoyed such rice. In all your lives you may never eat anything like it.' He looked as if he was drowning in an unearthly bliss.

Yet another, disgusted with this story, said angrily, 'Let me assure you that you are not the only one to have feasted on such rice. I too ate rice like this four years ago in Channapatna.' Then the others began to pull his leg, wondering aloud whether he was really remembering a true past, and managed to silence him with their laughter. Their merriment attracted more and more people.

Back at home, the women were getting ready, finding all sorts of containers to collect tomorrow's harvest, seeing all the while the dishes they could cook with the harvested paddy. The little children collapsed with sleep on the shoulders of the elders. The men smoked their beedis, cursing the fact that their women never cooked tasty dishes.

Meanwhile Thopamma, the bazaar harlot, thought of the ragi hittu* she had borrowed from every house in the colony. She began to calculate: out of the paddy gathered tomorrow, I can pay back one seer of paddy for every quarter seer of ragi hittu I have borrowed; then I will have cleared all my debts.

The champion toddy-drinker of the town, Chilre,* was making his own calculations: Somehow I must grab some five bags of paddy during the harvest tomorrow; then sell them, put the money in the coconut business, and ensnare the widow Janakavva into my net!

The entire colony warmed with dreams; with a hundred plans. Then they all went to bed, hoping and believing that at last their empty, wasted lives would be filled with riches. Their bodies felt the cool breeze from the plain, a breeze that travelled across the wide fields and wafted in with the aroma of paddy.

The town's pond, which had turned into a plain, had been transformed into a fertile field thanks to the yearly sedimentation of earth over it. The landlords who owned land adjacent to Olagere plain began to encroach into the fertile Olagere fields. Some of their own caste fumed. They owned land further away; they did not have the benefit of water and they harvested nothing. Then someone sent an anonymous petition to the government about the illegal encroachment.

---

ragi hittu: millet flour
Chilre: the name is a pun as chilre also means small change

The tehsildar, who always responded promptly to such developments, used all his official powers and acted immediately. This efficient officer welcomed such challenges. He thought tackling them was historically necessary to bring about justice in the country. An official proclamation was issued to say that this time the government was confiscating the crop of the fields in the dried-up pond, because it had been illegally cultivated. Though the officer's predecessor had issued a notice against this illegal act, it had been ignored; this time the government meant business and would itself harvest the crop. At the same time, the government went ahead with its programme of reviving the public pond.

An official statement was also issued to say that the government would employ people of that colony as labour to harvest the crop; this was the tehsildar's own decision. The tehsildar announced that people would be allowed to take home as much of the crop as they could harvest. All this was announced to the village through the official drummer, rousing the colony to feverish activity. Everyone was waiting for dawn to break!

It seemed that even the cocks responded to their anxious anticipation, and crowed the coming of day sooner than they should have. Some got up even earlier, with lit beedis between their lips. They had never had a day like this to wake up to. Their lifelong dreams — of sumptuous heaps of rice — seemed to have finally come true.

The illegal owners of the fields, taken by surprise by the sudden announcements, seemed helpless for the time being. The other landlords didn't care; they had nothing to lose.

As the morning light wrapped itself round the colony like a warm cloth, they sprang to action. Their scythes stirred with metallic sounds. Muttanna was dreaming of the huge heaps of paddy that would be his reward for his labour. Almost everything, objects both likely and unlikely, were grabbed to collect the paddy: baskets, bags, blankets, rugs, even old saris.

Thopamma was running around with a piece of cloth, urging the womenfolk, 'Come on, you whores. What are you waiting for? Are you going to sit there dumb, waiting for fortune to knock on your doors?' Even the little boys were getting ready to collect the paddy. Many of

them had forgotten to eat last night's leftovers, and were content with
the jaggery-sweetened tea from the shop. The very old felt disappointed
that God had cheated them of being part of the harvest.

The pond area now bustled with activity and noise as if a fair or festival
was on. Everybody marched toward the site. The residents of the upper
colony were amazed at the size and solidarity of the scythes held lovingly
in their hands, and the unearthly courage and spirit that lit their faces.

They moved fast. The boys ran as if they were buses, ahead of the
adults. The sun rose in the sky. Everybody was carrying something, and
Thopamma was urging them to gallop ahead. The men moved with giant
steps to reach the fields; in their midst Chilre shouted something like a
message. As they walked along the banks of the fields, the sunlight fell
on them, so that the shadows of what they carried moved along with
them.

They stood dumbstruck for a moment as their eyes took in the
expanse of the fields and the glistening gold of the paddy crop. No one
could have captured the countless emotions that crowded their faces.
Young boys touched the hanging paddy stalks gently, like birds, with
unconcealed joy.

By now the tehsildar too had arrived, flanked by police constables;
they positioned themselves in the shade of a tree. There was no sign of
the illegal field-owners. Their womenfolk stood at a safe distance, hurling
curses at the harvesters. But the hopes and desires of the harvesters
danced along with the paddy crop swaying gently in the breeze.

The tehsildar addressed the gathering, 'Look here. No one should
make any unnecessary noise. Cut the crop in complete silence. Organize
yourselves efficiently by dividing the work. Don't be afraid of being
attacked. But you must finish the harvesting today. You must also finish
beating the paddy by this evening.' His words provided the signal for
the epic event to start.

They stepped into the slushy fields. They began cutting the crop at
an incredible speed, their scythes waving and swishing, their bangles
jangling, wielding their tools with dexterity. The harvesters' footsteps
on the slushy ground looked like thousands of drawings. Since they

could not use scythes, young boys picked paddy bunches with their hands and stored them in their small bags. The work was divided spontaneously, on the spot. Some collected the cut paddy and heaped it, while others poured the paddy into bags for beating and winnowing. Yet others heaped the stalks in one place. It was marvelous teamwork, carried out with exemplary speed and skill. Sweat streamed down from their rhythmically moving bodies. Large parts of the field were being harvested at great speed.

Chilre rushed around, as if he was directing everybody, meddling in everyone else's work; all the while scheming ways of filching three bundles of paddy for himself. He screamed, 'Faster, faster, you have no time to wipe your sweat! Don't forget that the Sahib wants us to finish everything by this evening.'

Those who made bundles of the paddy were amazed; they had never before collected so much paddy. The tehsildar, enjoying the sight of so many people working so fast, and with such enthusiasm, chatted with his colleagues underneath a tree.

In a few hours, the cut paddy rose in huge heaps. Nearby, the paddy was beaten and winnowed in the wind, then packed into bags placed in a neat row. All the time the paddy fields were being emptied of the crop. Women, their saris unselfconsciouly tucked up to their thighs, wielded their scythes. No one had the time to enjoy the spectacle of their thighs melting with sweat. The little boys were taking the bags to their homes. Some sneaked away extra bags.

The scorching sun blazed in the sky. The police felt jealous when they saw how quickly the people worked. Even they couldn't have lathi-charged with such speed if they had been ordered to do so by their superiors! Nobody knew where the illegal land-owners had fled. Though they felt some fear deep down, the harvesters also felt safe working under the protective eyes of the constables. By now, all of them had succeeded in taking away quite a bit of paddy. In spite of this, the paddy heaps grew sky-high. As the fields emptied, the winnowed husk turned into a large hill.

That evening, even as they dreamt of her, the bewitching enchantress lay abjectly at their feet. Their bodies and clothes were crumpled and exhausted. They looked different now; the men's arms and the women's waists showed the most signs of exhaustion. Hunger had fled from them, ashamed of itself. The work went on, almost automatically, and most of the fields had been harvested. It was growing dark, but people were still taking the paddy home. Chilre, after stealthily maneuvering five bundles of paddy to the sugarcane field of the village headman, stood there triumphant, scanning the expansive paddy field that lay there, emptied of everything.

Then there was a disruption, as if to say that there are always forces to hinder or control human effort. The tehsildar was jolted by the picture he saw at a distance. The people greeted the new arrivals with total incomprehension. The arrivals were the Deputy Commissioner of the district, the Police Circle Inspector, other minions of officialdom, and naturally, the illegal owners of the fields. The atmosphere changed with the suddenness of lightning, as if someone unknown had twisted the throat of all that was living and eager there.

The Deputy Commissioner angrily took the tehsildar to task. The illegal landowners watched silently, wincing when they saw the heaps of paddy staring at them. Here and there hostile words were exchanged. The constables who had come there to protect the harvesters were now totally confused.

The tehsildar insisted in his officialese English, 'No sir, I did it legally.'

The Deputy Commissioner also rapped out in English, as if to silence a subordinate, 'Who said it is legal action? It is just a cruel action against village people and I know what kind of idiot you are.'

The colony residents didn't know what to do.

The Deputy Commissioner lapsed into Kannada, 'Out of love for your own untouchables you have done this and destroyed the village peace. I know what action should be taken against you.'

He turned his furious face to the landlords. They reeled off a long list of crimes supposedly committed by the tehsildar. Then the DC ranted that his subordinate had allowed the untouchables to harvest the paddy without his written permission. The tehsildar had indeed written to the

DC about it, but had acted without waiting for written permission. The landlords shouted that the tehsildar himself was an untouchable and that his action was partial to the interests of his community.

Then they let loose a flood of abuse against all untouchables.

The harvesters felt trapped. They wondered how to get out of the situation; they tried to steal away.

The uppercaste landlords moved forward with energy and opened their mouths wide to hurl a legal point, 'Show us the law which says we should give half the harvested paddy to the untouchables!' They complained loudly that the labourers were now getting away; that they had stored the entire crop in their homes; that they had recklessly harvested from adjacent, legally-owned fields; that the whole harvesting was a caste-motivated affair; and that the tehsildar had to take full responsibility for the outbreak of violence.

The poor tehsildar did not know how to face the accusations heaped on him. The fields, full of slush, stared at them. The harvesting crowd began to melt.

As evening drew near, their problems grew like tails. Three of the illegal landlords had seized land belonging to the untouchables. These farmers had not yet harvested their crop. The landlords now pointed to those lands and said, 'See, sirs, how they have not touched the crop in the lands of their own untouchables.' The constables remained silent. The Circle Inspector walked up and down solemnly. The landlords cried revenge, demanding that the tehsildar be dismissed and the untouchables punished. Night crept in slowly.

The anti-climax took place like this: Before the harvest, the landlords rushed to Bangalore, hobnobbed with the politicians there, bought their support and then won the support of the DC and other officers. It was a well-organized counter-move. The fact that the tehsildar did not have written permission was blown up. The now united landlords placed a proposal before the officers. First, the untouchables should bring back the paddy they had stored in their houses; if they did not want to return the paddy it could officially be counted as levy. It could also be adjusted against the landlords' irrigation debts to the government. The officials accepted these suggestions.

The paddy-dream of the untouchables now collapsed, like a silver bird falling to the ground when its wings are clipped.

The landlords who had not been affected also joined their aggrieved brothers. No one knew where the anonymous sender of the petition against illegal cultivators had gone. The entire colony was in the grip of anguish. The poor tehsildar too was nowhere to be found.

The sun had yet to sink below the horizon. The dream of the people was not yet dead. They struggled desperately to salvage it by stashing away as much of the paddy as they could. They filled all sorts of containers, and hid them in all sorts of unlikely places! Mayamma thought up an ingenious scheme. She cooked the paddy in a huge pot, thinking she could save it by claiming it was hers. And she was sure it would be impossible for them to retrieve the cooked paddy. Some of her neighbours firmly believed that any constable who dared enter her hut with boots on would start vomiting blood. Chilre's mind was aflame. The local Gnaneshwar Sangha, a youth organization, was unable to stir up any protest. Manchavva dragged a bundle of paddy to the backyard, and hid it in a small vessel covered with odds and ends. As she squatted on the floor, she tried to contain her racing heart.

Everyone seemed involved in a struggle to save something momentous. They covered the mouths of the paddy-filled vessels with wet saris to make it appear they were spread to be dried. Some were frustrated that they couldn't hide the paddy in their huts. While the small boys were befuddled by their elders' helplessness, older girls sat crumpled in a corner, overcome with shame and fear. The youth of the colony sat on the steps of a college near the public circle, gossiping, as if what was happening was none of their business.

Suddenly the colony was electrified by a new excitement. They were no longer concerned with a fistful of paddy; they were drawn into something larger, the need to defend their undefined rights. The police constables and officials had begun to invade the colony to retrieve the harvested paddy. The whole colony lay immersed in a sea of darkness, paralysed. It was as if it was night; or that the sun had died; or as if all

vitality and courage could be killed by petty intrigue and humiliation.

The official party entered the colony, determined that the untouchables should surrender the hidden paddy; else they would see that not
a grain remained with them. Since the DC was there to supervise the
operation, the constables had to act quickly and efficiently. The Circle
Inspector too was under pressure to perform his duty well. He was in
line for a promotion and had to impress the DC.

He ordered the constables around, shouting, 'Rush in. Search every
nook and corner and load the hidden paddy on to the lorry waiting
outside.'

The people began to tremble with fear.

The Inspector roared his order like a government lion, 'Come on,
charge!'

The helpless constables who had been asked to protect the harvesters
in the morning were now ordered to attack them and recover the paddy.
They were confused and hesitant, but finally they rushed into the houses.
Some of the men stood in their way and pleaded, 'Please sir, don't enter
our huts with your boots on and insult our gods.' Small children scurried
away to hide. Old women came forward to touch their feet and plead.
Someone broke into a sob. Everywhere the word Rush was heard. When
they found they were being resisted, the constables had no choice but
to use their lathis.

An enraged Chilre danced in anguish, 'Sir, beat us to death. After all,
your lathis, boots and guns are meant to be used against poor, small folk
like us. Kill us and bury us here. Like that paddy, destroy the colony of
untouchables.'

The constables rushed like demons into the huts and pulled out the
hidden paddy. The widow Thopamma stood there, intending to take
them on and teach them a lesson. She was the only mid-wife in the entire
village. She was always there to console and help people when there was
misfortune and death. But now the tears collected in her eyes and she
hesitated to come out.

The paddy grains fallen between boot-shod feet looked forlorn. The constables looked ferocious when they smashed pots with their lathis, or tumbled containers so that the grain rolled noisily on to the floor. They rushed about as if they were mad, hunting for the hidden paddy. Now the people grovelled on the ground. The men ran helter-skelter, fearing imprisonment. The women's dreams had been dashed to the ground like their pots and containers. Meanwhile, the paddy cooking in Mayamma's hut sent out a pleasant aroma that reached the noses of the constables.

In Chamayya's house they threw out coconuts along with the paddy. Only the day before yesterday he had stored the stolen coconuts. Seeing them, someone said, 'Look sirs, who knows what else these thieves have hidden inside?' This set off an even more thorough house-search, and along with the paddy, they began to seize anything they suspected was stolen. All sorts of things were found in all sorts of houses. The very body of the untouchables' colony was being stripped naked.

The constable with the pot-belly shouted, 'Bring out whatever else you have hidden. Otherwise the whole village may be arrested. We can find even buried corpses. So you better take things out yourself.'

When she heard this, Manchavva dragged out the paddy bundle she had hidden in the backyard, panting, and threw it before them. She wailed, beating her mouth, and then simply vanished. The constable had not yet reached Mayamma's house where she was cooking the paddy in a big pot. Poor Chilre's paddy bundles were stolen by someone who must have watched him hide them. But Chilre did not know this yet. One of the landlords flaunted his shiny moustache and accused them of crime after crime, going on and on as if he was going to recite all the crimes ever committed on earth! The colony's school-boys grew angry but they blamed the residents. 'Who the devil asked them to do it? Let them suffer.' Then they fell silent and kept to themselves.

In the search party was an untouchable constable. He went about pretending to perform his duty. The constable who entered Mayamma's hut got angry when he couldn't find the paddy. 'So this is your plan, you old hag,' he shouted, kicking the pot on the stove. The pot rolled down and the cooked grains of paddy scattered, filling the hut with its mouth-watering aroma. As the aroma spread everywhere, Mayamma sobbed and cursed with the same breath, but she couldn't do anything about the spilt paddy. Some said, as they watched all this, 'Even if our children starved, died of hunger and became rotten corpses, we wouldn't want to touch this paddy.' They gave up the paddy they had stored so carefully.

The paddy fell outside in a heap. The officials couldn't believe that so much had been stolen! But they were pleased with their success. His hands crossed over his belly, a fuming Chilre stood silent, watching. Then he saw a constable fleeing Thopamma's house.

About four days back, Thopamma had carved beef out of a slaughtered bullock. After eating some of it, she had cut up the rest, strung the pieces into a garland, and hung them out to dry before being preserved. But the pieces had not dried properly and had begun to rot, swarming with worms and flies. They stank horribly. To resist the policeman who rushed into her house, the only weapon she could lay her hands on were the bits of beef. She thrust them on the nose of the policeman and had him running for his life to escape the killing stench. Then Thopamma ran out and gave the DC the same treatment, spoiling his white clothes. Some of the officials ran away, but a few constables rushed at her, caught her and tied her up after a beating. With this success the anger of the officials doubled. They saw what had happened as a challenge to their authority and honour. The Sub-Inspector ordered a lathi-charge. Then they beat everyone without restraint so that not a creature was left in the ransacked hovels.

The fact that a mere woman could wield garlands of rotting meat and humiliate him made the Circle Inspector think deeply. He felt the situation must have wider dimensions, beyond the local and the immediate; there must have been a plan to resist the official party. Of course, it was obvious that some external agency must have had a hand in all this. The more he thought, the more convinced he became that the old woman's act was distinctly naxalite in style! And the landlords said a local untouchable youth studying in Bangalore had returned last year to organize a group, the Gnaneshwar Sangha. Their suspicions reinforced, the officials were now convinced the whole thing was a naxalite operation. They began to worry about setting up a different kind of enquiry into the incident.

In the thickness of night, the members of the Sangha were arrested by the landlords. Chilre tried to hide in the darkness. Paddy had taken the village into a complex political conspiracy; the colony was the centre of an armed rebellion. The incident became a serious political issue. Some landlords who had lost in the recent elections tried to give it a new twist. They said there were organized attempts to disrupt the peace of the village and that threats to life had increased. As a result, Thopamma and the others were arrested and taken in a police van to Channapatna. They were described as reckless, violent terrorists. No one knew where the paddy collected by the colony had gone. In any case the residents had lost all interest in it. They were now in the grip of something deeper — the tragedy of living a life that had become a relentless hunt. The visiting official party soon left the village and got busy with follow-up action. Thopamma refused to say anything, remained monumentally silent, and prepared for the worst as she was hustled into the van. Chilre planned to get his friends released on bail after selling paddy to the Muslim merchants in Honganur.

Daylight woke like an epileptic in the sleeping colony. Men squatted here and there, smoking beedis as if nothing had happened. The crows cawed as if they were cursing. No one had eaten the night before, and their bellies suffered in the early morning heat, hunger jostling with humiliation. They hoped that the landlords in the upper colony would give them some coolie work, though they also knew that this was impossible. The upper caste men had resolved that very night to teach the colony residents a lesson by not employing them.

As the sun rose, the women mopped up the night's wreckage of broken pots and vessels. The village was buried in complete silence. Then a constable arrived from the town. This scared them, though he was one of those who had come earlier with the tehsildar to protect the harvesters. He called a few people and they sat in one of the front-yards, talking.

They questioned him, full of fear, curiosity and shame.

He told them that when the arrested villagers were being taken in the van, Thopamma had managed to slip out and escape. The senior officers had then sent a constable to the village to capture her immediately. An uncomfortable but sympathetic constable appealed to the people to hand her over if they saw her. He also warned the villagers that the officers may take drastic action against their boys in Bangalore.

Chilre said to him, 'Why should you suffer for our misfortune, sir? We know how to ripen our suffering and eat the fruit.'

No one had the energy or strength to react. They now knew what that witch, paddy, had brought upon them after her tantalizing dance; they could only squat now, in a stillness marked by exhaustion, hunger, anguish and humiliation.

When he had made sure that Thopamma was not there, the constable left the village. In the eyes of the colony the image of Thopamma grew and grew till it appeared a supernatural force. In their dreams, they now looked hopefully to her arrival.

As time passed, people melted into their own shadows. Mayamma's grandson, unable to bear his hunger, began picking up the cooked paddy grains scattered around the stove. He stuffed his little mouth with them. He chewed hard, spat out the husk; the paddy juice streamed from the two corners of his mouth. It seemed as if he could digest everything.

The whole village was steeped in a profound silence, as it stuffed its belly with all sorts of things. They felt the wind blow from the dried pond fields, where their hopes of a harvest lay dead. And time, bearing its burden of truths in its womb, grew and grew.

Translated by K. Raghavendra Rao

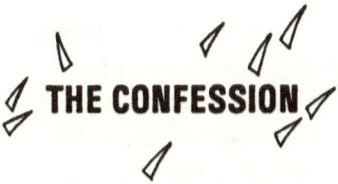

THE CONFESSION

VAIDEHI

Even now, Narmada wakes up in the night, startled, when she remembers. She sits up all of a sudden, feeling sick. She too should tell someone. But whom?

It was nothing really. That woman, the one who had got into the train as it was leaving, sat quietly, like a black stone. She would have been scary if seen in the dark. But she didn't look evil . . . Even now, how could one call her wicked? Or a coward? Or honest, bad, truthful, ungrateful? She seemed to be all these. Or she was each one of these at different times. But that day she did seem like a woman sitting quietly after having gulped down something.

Her husband said to her once again, after she had got on to the train and sat down, 'Narmada, send a telegram as soon as you get there.'

'Yes.'

'No. Send one even before that. Just to say where you are. No, no. Send telegrams from wherever you can.'

'Yes.' Both of them smiled. 'You act as if we were married only the other day. If you feel so bad, don't send me alone. Come with me.'

'No,' he said, 'You go. But don't stay back because of the children. Give my good wishes to the new couple . . .'

He got off the train and stood outside. 'Send a telegram to tell me how the children are.' (He was all love, inside and outside.)

Till he left, she hadn't even seen the woman. Or if she had, the fact hadn't sunk in.

The train moved. He went out of sight. Narmada arranged her things in the compartment to make herself comfortable. She felt the loneliness that enveloped her once he had left; she absorbed it, letting it sink into her being as if coming to terms with reality.

It was then that she saw the woman clearly. As she looked, she felt she had seen those eyes somewhere before. Slowly, a fear overcame her. Where had she seen her? She felt bewildered as she tried to remember and her memories got mixed up. Those eyes, no, even the way they looked at her, was familiar. But there was no recognition in them. The woman smiled at Narmada in a friendly way.

'I thought I was alone. I'm glad to find you here.'

'I feel the same way,' said Narmada, more out of force of habit than with genuine feeling. Even though the woman was wearing a sari, it was draped around her so tightly that it didn't look like one. Her body was like that, big and broad, utterly shapeless, like a flat board.

'Was that your husband?' asked the woman.

'Yes.'

'Are you going home?'

'Yes.'

'Why? Anything special?'

The children stayed there. They went to school from their grandfather's. They were on holiday now. They should have come over but her sister was getting married and she had to go. It was tough to be away from the children. But there was no alternative. Their education shouldn't suffer. Another three years and her husband and she would go back. Until then, the children would stay with her parents.

Narmada answered each question in detail. Did the woman get a little worked up?

'If you really look at it, there are only three things in the world that matter — father, mother and child. Don't you agree?' she asked. The woman seemed to be hiding elsewhere even as she talked. As if she felt she had to keep talking. Otherwise the train wouldn't move!

'I heard your husband telling you to send a telegram.' She laughed. Her laughter seemed smeared with pain. 'Aren't some men really scared? Whatever you may say, it is only in India that men love women like children. Nowhere else . . . I am not talking about bad husbands — they are excluded of course . . .' Sorrow trembled in these last words.

Narmada spoke even though she noticed this. So that the woman would not discover her efforts to seek out the eyes that she couldn't place, she surrendered to speech.

'Yes. I'm his child. And he is mine. Isn't that what marriage is all about? In the beginning, husband, wife and child. Later, the same people are father, mother and child. As they grow older, they become grandfather, grandmother and grandchild. Other relationships come along, break, loosen, and they go looking for new relationships. But marriage is not like that. It goes on like this until death. If they get to know each other, understand and accept each other's stupidity and cleverness and carry on with a sense of give and take . . .' Narmada searched her memory for those eyes as she went on with her lecture. But it was impossible to look straight into them. They would escape! As if they were running away from all human beings . . .

, 'Yes!' said the woman. 'Your eyes became moist thinking of your husband. It is like that for me too. When I think of something good, the tears come to my eyes. It happens even when I think of something rotten. Why, if I were just to remember my mother! Look here!'

Her eyes were tearful but wouldn't focus anywhere, at anything. I have seen those eyes somewhere . . . Narmada was restless.

The woman told her mother's story.

Her mother's story was no different from that of any other mother in the world. Everywhere there are determined mothers who bring up their children against all odds and help them to settle down. In a way, it would be quite correct to say that the details of their hardships make up the history of the human race! This woman's mother had also lost her husband at an early age and become homeless. She suffered beyond description, made a human being of her daughter, got her married and sent her far away. Now, towards the end of her life, she lay ill in a small house in her son-in-law's property. She could barely get up. Her daughter, her son-in-law and grandchildren were all far away . . .

The woman said she was on her way back now from her mother's place. Why had she left her mother behind? There was no other way out. Her husband didn't get along with her mother. Her mother was old and a little fussy by nature. She could tolerate her. But he? And it wasn't just that. Her mother too didn't want to leave the place where she had grown up. Her last days, the soil from which she grew . . . all that was there of course! That's why she came over once in two months, stayed for a fortnight, provided her mother with everything she needed and then went back to her husband. Her mother had had a nurse to look after her for the last three years!

A woman who had fought and been defeated. When Narmada said, 'I'm sorry. What a predicament,' the woman sighed and said, 'Yes. How can I say it's a predicament? On the whole . . .' But why did her eyes escape as if to hide something? As if they cried aloud that there was no relief if it was not revealed, as if they were wandering in search of a place where it could be revealed?

The train moved on, like time. For thoughts that run like a train, there are no tracks. In the end all thoughts merge together, become a hotchpotch and sleep oozes out . . . Narmada sat up startled. The woman was right next to her. She trembled with such fear that she was about to scream 'Amma!' but she controlled herself. She asked instead, 'What is it? What do you want?'

The woman didn't speak. She just sat there, like a black stone, blinking, without smiling or crying, just dull.

'What is it? ' asked Narmada, shaking her. She lifted up the face . . . and looked at her eyes. Goodness! Where had she seen them? In that lesson! At the elementary school! Can anyone say how or when something learnt in childhood will crop up? Weren't these the eyes of the barber's wife? The one whose husband had said the king's ears were donkey's ears? They were exhausted eyes, unable to hold what was inside. How did they come here? Narmada was amused; and when she looked down at the woman's stomach, it seemed bloated. It was obese; it would look like that always.

Narmada laughed aloud. 'Good God! How scared I was when I saw you! Because I had seen those eyes somewhere. But really . . .

these . . . they belong to a story I read in my childhood.'

The woman too should have laughed, considering how heartily Narmada laughed. Like everything else, this too was a habit, laughing even when you don't feel like it. But she sat there, silent, as if she was beyond that habit. Then suddenly, taking hold of Narmada's hand, she began sobbing.

'I shall tell . . . I shall . . . everything.'

'Why are you weeping? What happened?'

'If I tell you, promise me you won't tell anyone else. No, I can't talk about it to anyone at home. Not even to my husband.'

Narmada watched her quietly. She seemed to have been weakened by rushing up and down every two months, over many years. And behind this rushing about was the movement between two minds. A tired, worn-out woman who was like a link that couldn't be severed from either this side or the other . . . What could she say? It was only right to take her mother home with her now. Did she feel like this because she burnt inside at the thought of her mother with the nurse, in a house that belonged to a son-in-law who could not live with her? How could he love her mother when he was so irritated by her? The children who noticed how they lived by themselves, leaving her lonely, helpless mother to herself . . . Was there a fear of what they would do in the future? No. None of this matched the depths of thought in those eyes.

'It's all right. Whatever it is, tell me, if it's going to make you feel better. I don't know who you are. I won't tell anyone . . .'

'I don't know what you will say when you hear it. Do you understand? Do you smell blood on my body? Listen, listen to me. This time when I went there, I finished off my mother. I killed her. Are you listening? I strangled her as she slept. I cremated her and finished everything. I don't need to go there anymore. There is no one there . . . Amma will forgive me . . . she will, won't she?'

Narmada sat still.

'Tell me! Who should I have killed? Myself? My husband? Or . . .?'

The train stopped at some town or the other. The woman, who had earlier said she would be getting off at a place some distance away, got down in a great hurry, leaving Narmada behind. Narmada sat, unmoving, silent, bewildered. It was still dark . . .

There was a noise at the door. Had she come back? Startled, Narmada looked up and saw a couple holding a baby. They caressed it tenderly as they walked in, like proud people walking in with a whole beautiful world in their arms.

Narmada screamed softly and clutched the window bars for support. The train dashed along, howling like a demon.

Translated by Padma Ramachandra Sharma

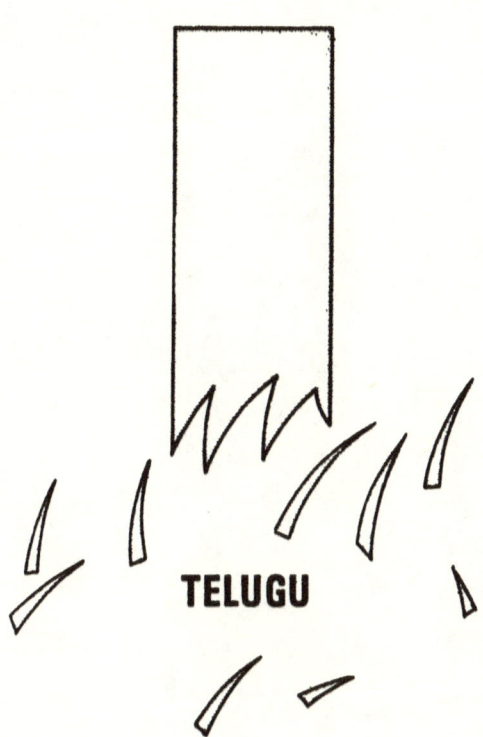

TELUGU

INTRODUCTION

The short story, one of the most popular forms in recent Telugu literature, is a modern product, expressing contemporary ideas and evoking contemporary sensibilities. At a rough estimate, over three thousand Telugu short stories appear every year in periodicals and magazines that cater to an expanding reading public — a readership with some leisure, a taste for fiction, and possibly an inclination for better institutions — political, legal, social and cultural. This is not to deny the sizeable sections of a middle-class readership who respond best to 'entertainers' or pulp; perhaps an inevitable situation in a highly commercialised social context. It is sad but realistic to acknowledge that close to two-thirds of what is published falls into the pulp category.

Leaving the negative aspect of the picture aside, the Telugu short story has been, from its beginnings in 1910, consistent in its attempts to create, evoke and refine the modern sensibilities of its readers. A host of writers from Gurajada (1862-1915) onwards were inspired by the social, political and literary movements of the time, including the social reform movement, the nationalist movement, the leftist movements, and the romantic, progressive and radical literary movements.

Succeeding generations of writers continued to be influenced by Gurajada's legacy of realism, a legacy that was manifested in many forms including 'reform realism,' 'critical realism' and 'progressive realism.' Among the important writers of the first generation whose work revealed this influence were Sripada Subramania Shastri, Chalam, Karuna Kumara, Gopichand, K. Kutumba Rao, Padmaraju, Buchibabu, Chaso and Ratchakonda Viswanatha Shastri. The second generation, including writers such as Kalipatnam Rama Rao, Madhurantakam Rajaram, Vasireddy Sitadevi and Ranganayakamma, carried on the tradition; followed by a growing number of writers in the third and fourth generations. (It might be relevant to note here that the works of several of these writers are not available in translation, either in other Indian languages or in English.)

The four stories in this collection, all recently written, can be read with this heritage in mind. Among other things they reflect the continuing preoccupation with social realism, and the emphasis on rural life as both theme and setting.

Swamy's 'Vana Rale' ('Rain') and Chakravenu's 'Kuwait Savitramma' are based on the rural life of the Southern Andhra region, Rayalaseema. Allam Rajaiah's story, 'Manishi Lopali Vidwamsam' ('The Desolation Within'), describes the villages of Telengana in Northern Andhra. Abburi Chaya Devi's 'The Woodrose' is the only one of the four stories that has a metropolitan setting.

The images of rural life presented in 'Rain,' 'Kuwait Savitramma' and 'The Desolation Within' are startling and disturbing; they are also starkly realistic. In 'Rain' we see a continuous conflict between man and nature — a hopeless battle that the tillers in the story engage in, and ironically enough, with hope. We also see, side by side with this one-sided battle, human relationships changed, debased to the level of mere trade. The central image of the story is a picture of semi-arid, rain-fed lands in Anantapur District of Southern Andhra, lands dependent on the vagaries of the monsoon and the manipulations of the marketplace for its cultivation. The note of quiet despair at the end of the story is a natural conclusion given the story as it is built up to that point.

The picture is somewhat different in the Northern Andhra districts described in 'The Desolation Within.' These areas, especially in and around the villages of the coal belt, are reeling under abject poverty, a corrupt bureaucracy and the widespread consumption of liquor; in short, under dehumanized conditions. The eventual reaction to such a situation is, as implied in the story, an active naxalite movement. Rajaram, the son of a farmer, 'weeps at the crossroads, in the cold, in the dark, in hunger, in grief, for the son he has lost and for all that was his and that he has lost.'

Who will understand the desolation within Rajaram? asks the author Allam Rajaiah at the end of the story. Rajaiah ends the story with this question, along with a suggestion of a possible answer; a suggestion in the shape of a symbol. All the scenes and episodes that go before, scenes that starkly reveal the desolation of the pauperized peasants, lead up to this point.

A word on the structure of the story. It has the structure of a novel within the short story form. The different episodes — the Rajesam-related episodes and the Rajaram-related episodes — do not seem well-connected; but they do, taken together, achieve the desired emotional intensity.

'Kuwait Savitramma' and 'The Woodrose' are centred around their female protagonists. The increasing interest in women-related themes in the recent Telugu short story may be partly traced back to the social reform movements; it is also a reflection of a marked rise in the number of women writers and readers. 'Kuwait Savitramma' deals with the poverty and helplessness of villagers. In such situations they may have to tear asunder all the bonds familiar to them, both patriarchal and cultural. A paradox is well-knit into the story: the brother-in-law who rapes Savitramma and then ensures through the village panchayat that she leaves the village, later sends his wife to Kuwait with Savitramma. This story indicates the erosion of the moral base and the cultural supremacy of the joint family. The status of women has been reduced to the level of a commodity by the husbands themselves. The author Chakravenu depicts, through details about Savitramma's village, the disintegration of feudal hegemony, and the different faces of wealth and social status. The story, beginning with a flashback, has a neat structure; and a tone which has an undercurrent of both pathos and righteous indignation.

'The Woodrose' tackles an entirely different and more obviously middle-class concern: the problem of dependent old women, who are painfully aware of the 'difference between growing old in the village and growing old in the town' or a city. The perennial problem of the relationship between the old and the young, and between a grown-up son and a now dependent old mother, has been treated with sensitivity through the old woman's monologue in realistic, conversational language.

In 'The Woodrose,' standard modern Telugu is used in both the old woman's interior monologue as well as her conversation with others. In 'Kuwait Savitramma' and 'The Desolation Within,' the standard dialect is used in the narrative, and the different regional dialects in speech styles. Only 'Rain' uses the regional dialect for narration as well as speech styles. Both combinations are effective in the creation of atmosphere and locale, in placing the stories geographically, hence culturally. The regional dialect is, in addition, used to advantage to flesh out individual characters. The rich legacy of the oral tradition is also consciously and effectively interwoven with the language used in both 'Rain' and 'The Desolation Within.' The use of regional dialects and the oral tradition has, in fact, become part of the realistic short story in recent times. This trend is indicative of a new assertiveness in contemporary Telugu writing, a confidence that is largely the result of leftist and democratic political and literary movements.

Kethu Viswanatha Reddy

RAIN

SWAMY

Pennappa pricked up his ears at the patel's words. 'The government has announced on All-India Radio, that we'll have good rains this year. A good monsoon!'

The village patel was talking to the peasants who had gathered round him for news. 'Some other people too are saying the same thing,' he concluded.

Hope fluttered somewhere deep within Pennappa's breast when he heard the patel's words. And though many of the peasants gathered there were sceptical, Pennappa decided to throw caution to the winds.

A few days later, Pennappa got up at the crack of dawn and had a good oil bath. He asked his wife to oil and comb his thick, unruly hair. He wore freshly-washed clothes and a neat shoulder-cloth. It was almost as if he was dressed up for a festival! Then he set out for the neighbouring town of Chellikara.

He made straight for the shop dealing with agricultural produce and arrived just as the price of groundnut was being discussed. His mouth fell open in shock and amazement.

'One thousand rupees?' he exclaimed. 'How can it be one thousand rupees, Sahukar? Last year we sold our groundnut seed to you for only seven hundred rupees. Is it fair to buy from us at seven hundred and sell it back to us at a thousand?'

'What can I do? Is it in my hands? That was the market rate then. This is the market rate now. Well, since you are arguing as cleverly as a lawyer in court, tell me something. Why did you sell all your groundnut last year without keeping some seeds to sow this year? That was not a very clever thing to do was it?' retorted the shopkeeper.

'You know quite well that we didn't even get a fourth of the normal crop,' Pennappa protested. 'And if I had put it away for this season's sowing, what would my family have eaten for the rest of the year? And how would we repay loans we have taken from people like you?'

'They sell the entire crop, blaming some kind of emergency or the other. Now they complain that the market rate is higher,' mumbled the shopkeeper under his breath.

Pennappa cursed his luck. It's all fate, he thought.

'All right, Pennappa.' The shopkeeper's voice broke into his reverie. 'How much seed do you want?'

For five acres one and a half bags will do. Pennappa started a quick calculation. For ten I will need three bags. But the price of seed . . . too much for someone like me. Should I sow just five acres and leave the other five fallow? Or should I take courage in my hands and buy enough seeds for ten acres? He was lost in the throes of indecision till he suddenly remembered the prediction of Poleramma, the goddess of the village. She had possessed Danayya and spoken through him. She had said it would rain. Surely the prediction of a deity cannot go wrong . . . He took a bold decision and bought three bags of seeds. After all there is a god above . . .

The shopkeeper was now very friendly. 'Look, Pennappa,' he said, 'when the crop is harvested, remember you must sell it all to me. You'll be doing me an injustice if you offer it to anyone else.'

When Pennappa reached home, his wife looked at him as if he had taken leave of his senses. Not one, not two but *three* bags of groundnut seed!

'This year no one is sure whether the rains will come. Haven't you seen that even the rich farmers are hesitant to sow? Why have you brought three bags of seed, swami? Suppose the rains are scanty like last year. Or it doesn't rain at all. If you sow all the seeds it will be like throwing the three thousand rupees down the drain. How will we repay the loan? How will we pay the interest? How do we eat? And have you forgotten?' Pennappa's wife paused. 'Have you forgotten? We were planning to get our daughter married next year. No, please swami, no! We don't want this wretched peasant's life and we don't need these unending debts. We'll live somehow. Get some work as a coolie-shoolie. When we earn some money, we'll eat. When we don't, we'll fill our stomach with water and starve.'

When Pennappa saw his wife weeping he began to lose his confidence. But he was not going to let her see it. So he began to shout at her.

'Tchah, you chicken-hearted whore! If I hear another inauspicious word I'll bash your face in! Has any man ever gained anything from the advice of women?'

His wife fell silent, sulking. But inside Pennappa, his bravado slowly ebbed away. Her words, 'We don't want this wretched peasant's life! We don't need these unending debts!' kept ringing in his ears.

I'll sow only five acres, he thought to himself. Let the other five remain fallow. Suppose the rains don't come. It's better to lose fifteen hundred rupees instead of three thousand.

Pennappa kept half the seed and sold the other half to Rangappa for the same price he had paid. His wife heaved a deep sigh of relief.

Looking forward to the rain, the peasants tilled the soil during Krittika. If it rained in Punarvasa, they could sow the seed.

They could see a few clouds but a strong wind soon blew them away across the skies. Not a single cloud came low enough for it to rain.

So many sins have heaped up in the world, thought Pennappa. How can we expect it to rain?

Punarvasa gave way to Pushyami. No rain.

Days passed.

No rain.

They celebrated the marriage of frogs. All in anticipation of rain.

No rain.

People recited the Vira Parva from the Mahabharata.

Still no rain.

At night the villagers went round the narrow lanes and by-lanes of the villages, carrying lanterns, singing bhajans. No rain.

Some of the young unmarried girls were asked to pour a hundred and one buckets of water on the sacred rock in the centre of the village. They broke a coconut at a special puja. But yet again, no rain.

What's to be done? thought a pensive Pennappa. He sat at the village bania's shop, chewing betelnut with four or five other peasants who had gathered there after the evening meal. They talked as they pulled slowly on their beedis.

'Hey, Penna!' they heard a loud voice. It was Lingappa. 'Look, you have seed for only five acres,' he said. 'I'll give you another one and a half bags so that you can sow the other five. What sin has that land committed that you let it lie fallow?'

Pennappa went out and spat a mouthful of betelnut and spittle. When he returned he looked at Lingappa with a sly smile on his face.

'You are offering me seeds, Lingappa, only because the rains have failed and you want to dump them on any fool who will buy them. Then you'll save at least on the interest. How shrewd you are! I have a better idea. Here, you take my one and a half bags of seed. I'll happily work for daily wages.'

'Our Penna is right. It's better to work as a coolie than to place our faith in this uncertain business of cultivation,' said Sankarappa, a farmer who was better off than most of them sitting there. He pulled at his beedi and told them, 'If any of you want seeds, come to me. I have eight bags.'

When Pennappa heard this, he sighed with relief. 'I did the right thing selling half the seed to Rangappa. If a well-off farmer like Sankarappa is beginning to lose heart, where do I go from here?'

'Cheer up, all of you,' said the bania. 'Look, all of you went to town spending good money on the fares. You bought the seed with borrowed money on which you have to pay interest. You bought it to sow your fields, not to give it away to someone else. Don't worry. It has to rain.'

Suddenly there was a lull. The wind stood still. They felt a sudden change in the weather. 'Chee! It's hot,' said the bania, wiping his hand on his vest. He went outside and looked at the sky.

'It's overcast,' he told them.

Lightning lit up the blackness of night.

Thunder rolled menacingly across the sky.

'Arjuna! Phalguna! Partha! Kiriti!' repeated Pennappa to himself to make sure he wasn't struck by lightning.

The talk now centred around rain.

'They say it has already rained two inches in the east. The entire land has turned green.'

'I believe they sowed their seeds during Arudra?'

'In fact, they had sown before Punarvasa set in. I wonder why they did it so early?'

'Where is the guarantee that it will rain again and again? They must have just put their faith in God and sown!'

'If it rains now, this is the right time to sow.'

'Yes, Punarvasa and Pushyami are good rainy months.'

'The other day, about a week ago, they say it rained heavily at Pillalapalli.'

'Yes. That rain was meant for us. Our village. But the wind blew the clouds towards Pillalapalli.'

'Fate, friend, fate! Until it rains, you can't say it has rained. Until we eat, the food is not ours.'

'Mama, I think it will definitely rain today.'

'Yes. I have that feeling too.'

As they were talking, a thin drizzle began to fall outside. Pennappa's hopes rose again.

Maybe there will be good rain now, he thought. Maybe this year I might just get a good crop. God knows whether I made a mistake giving Rangappa half the seeds. Maybe I would have been better off if I had sown all ten acres. One should never heed the talk of women. Wretched creatures! And he cursed his wife under his breath.

They all stepped out and stood gazing in the direction of the rain.

'Oh look! On Thimmappa Hill! See how heavily it's raining!'

'And look in the direction of Bommaganipalli. It's raining heavily there too.'

'The wind is blowing in our direction from the hill.'

'Krishna! Rama! Please send the rain to our village too. Dear God, I salute you with folded hands,' mumbled Pennappa.

But God was deaf. He didn't hear Pennappa's fervent prayer.

Suddenly the wind began to blow. The clouds that had been moving towards Teetakallu were now being blown away towards Pullikallu. Soon there was not a single cloud in the sky. Not a drop of rain. In a second, the sun was out shining bright and hot.

'Oh God, what have you done?' cried Pennappa to himself, lighting up a beedi. 'The sky was so cloudy. It was even beginning to rain and we were so full of hope. It's as if you brought a handful of food close to our mouths and then snatched it away, leaving us starving.'

Then he remembered his wife. 'Poor thing. I shouldn't have shouted at her. She was right. It was only because of her advice that I gave half the seed to Rangappa. At least I don't have to pay interest on that. She is not a chicken-hearted whore. I am a greedy bastard!'

Days passed.

Pushyami came and went.

Aslesha set in.

People lost hope.

'The time has gone. Even if it rains now, it will be of no use.'

Then two weeks after Aslesha set in, it began to rain.

'Why couldn't it have rained like this two weeks earlier?' asked the villagers, bemoaning their fate.

Even though it rained, many peasants did not have the courage to sow seeds at the end of Aslesha. Some kept hoping against hope for more rain, but they just could not decide whether to sow or not.

Those who had twenty acres sowed only ten. Those who had ten sowed five. Some decided not to sow at all.

Pennappa scattered seeds on five acres and left five fallow.

One week after sowing, the seeds sprouted. After two or three days, the seeds split into two halves. Each half looked like the frail wings of fledgling sparrows trying to fly.

In Magha it rained again. The farmers pulled out the weeds from the fields and went back to their ploughing.

Pubba came. The plants grew and started to flower. They were bedecked from head to toe in gold, like beautiful young girls just turning into women. A few more days and the plants grew bigger and stronger. Bees swarmed around the flowers. As a mother's face reflects her joy in her child, so the earth showed her pleasure in these healthy, growing plants.

Beside the lush field filled with the tender groundnut crop, the fallow field looked like a widow. But when the flowers began to drop, the peasant felt as happy as if he had been offered a plateful of cooked rice.

It didn't rain in Uttara.

Hasta came and went. And there was no rain.

At the end of the drop-roots, tender groundnuts began to form. At the same time, the earth was slowly beginning to lose its life-giving dampness. The plants began to die, slowly, agonisingly. They looked like young pregnant women who had been starving for days. The plants began to wilt and droop. Pennappa felt as if someone's hand had scooped out his insides.

A few days before Chitta was to pass and Swati was to set in, it drizzled for three days. The tiniest hope fluttered in Pennappa's heart. But it was short-lived.

Swati went by.

No rain.

Visakha came.

No rain.

Winter set in and with that Pennappa lost all hope of rain. The groundnut crop was poor. Only the drop-roots that had come out with the first rain were worth gathering. The second rain had produced nothing. And even among the gathered groundnuts not all of them were of the same size. Some had just withered and died in their shells like baby chicks that die before hatching. Pennappa gathered the crop and it did not even fill three bags. 'Oh God!' he cried in despair.

He asked everyone who returned from the neighbouring town about the rate of groundnut. One week they said the price was five hundred rupees per quintal, a couple of weeks later it was five hundred and fifty. Then it went up to six hundred. But fell again to five hundred and fifty.

These fluctuations didn't help Pennappa make up his mind. Should he hold out? Would the price go up again? He was like a matka gambler staying awake all night, waiting for the number to be declared.

One week the rate rose again to six hundred. Perhaps it will go up even more, thought Pennappa. But the next week it was down to five hundred. Rangappa sold his crop and returned to the village.

Pennappa was now afraid that the rate would fall even further if he delayed any longer. One day he loaded his three bags of crop on to a lorry and set off for the town.

The crop was weighed at the shop. But because of its poor quality, three bags of groundnuts weighed for a quintal instead of two and a half bags.

While weighing, three kilograms were reduced as wastage — sticks, broken shells and mud. When calculating the amount, the shopkeeper also deducted fifteen rupees towards the poor quality of the crop. Another rupee went to charity. Finally the shopkeeper deducted the loan and the interest on it.

Instead of giving him money, the shopkeeper dropped a small list of items in Pennappa's hand. Pennappa, who could not read or write, bent his head and looked at it closely. Then he asked the shopkeeper, 'So how much do I get in hand?'

'Nothing. In fact, you owe me eighty rupees,' said the shopkeeper softly.

Pennappa did not cry. He thought, I have lost eighty rupees cultivating five acres. If I'd cultivated ten acres, my loss would have been double. I'm certainly better off this way.

If I add the cost of labour — for me, my wife, my daughter and the bullocks — for five acres, it comes to about two thousand rupees. If I hadn't taken my wife's advice and cultivated another five acres it would have been four thousand. All that back-breaking labour would have been lost. I'm certainly better off. Then Pennappa laughed. A kind of mad, hysterical, unending laugh.

The shopkeeper thought Pennappa had gone mad.

When he stopped laughing, Pennappa asked the shopkeeper for a loan of thirty rupees.

Mad people did not ask for money, thought the shopkeeper, so he decided Pennappa was not mad after all. Poor fellow! he thought, taking out twenty rupees from his pocket. Together with the eighty Pennappa already owed, the debt was rounded off to a hundred rupees, and entered in a ledger against Pennappa's name.

'Take heart Pennappa,' said the shopkeeper sympathetically. 'Times won't always be this bad. There will be better days ahead.'

Pennappa remembered his elder daughter who had blossomed into womanhood three years ago.

He postponed her marriage to next year.

He thought of his wife's old blouse, frayed and torn at the shoulders.

He postponed the new blouse to next month.

He thought of his young son who had been clamouring for a slate. He postponed the slate to next week.

He suddenly realised he had not eaten a morsel since the morning. Rats gnawed at his stomach.

He postponed the hunger too till the next meal.

Having made these momentous decisions, he bought some dal, beedis and pounded rice. He tied it all into a bundle in a corner of his dhoti and boarded the bus for home on an empty stomach.

Days passed.

When there was work, he worked for daily wages.

When there was no work he sat on the temple steps, smoking his beedi and playing tiger and goat.

When people spoke of heavy rains thirty or forty years ago in this or that place and of rivers that ran in spate or lakes that overflowed, Pennappa listened in open-mouthed astonishment.

Arudra came once again.

Punarvasa entered.

Pennappa looked at the sky expectantly.

He listened to the weather forecast on Panchayati programmes for farmers.

He asked Danayya who was possessed by Poleramma whether it

would rain.

He asked the brahmin priest whether the new year would bring rain.

Should he sow five acres or ten acres this year? This time he must get seed well in time, he thought. Much before the rains set in.

Days passed slowly.

It was time again for the frogs' marriages.

The sky above stared down at Pennappa below in utter innocence.

Translated by Vijaya Ghose

THE WOODROSE

ABBURI CHAYA DEVI

Sitting in the balcony every evening and watching the passers-by has become a habit with me. What work do I have? My daughter-in-law looks after everything. When I go into the kitchen to do something, she says, 'What can you do? Please go and rest.'

When I wanted rest, I didn't have a moment's respite from the unending chores in the house. Now it is rest all the time till I am tired of it. I never thought old age would be so boring.

When I was younger, I thought being old would be a very happy time — relaxing in an easy-chair, playing with all the grandchildren, telling them stories, gossiping with neighbours, nagging everybody in the house, supervising all and sundry. Now that I am old I know better. I also know there is a big difference between growing old in the village and growing old in a town.

In this big city everyone is for himself; no one seems to care for others. The neighbours don't call on us and when they do, there is no informal air or intimacy. If we visit them, they are uncomfortable; they force a cup of coffee on us and see us off soon. So I thought it better to watch the passers-by from the balcony. That way some old and some new thoughts cross one's mind. That is as good a way as any to pass my time.

'What is it, Kamala?' I asked my daughter-in-law.

'I am planting the seed of a creeper,' she replied.

'What flowers? Are they sankham flowers?'

'No, this is called woodrose,' she said, still digging the earth.

I had never heard the name. These people call even chamanthi flowers by English names. Perhaps I knew these flowers already; I was curious; so I asked, 'What do they look like?'

'At first there are long, bell-shaped yellow flowers,' she said. 'Then from the middle of these flowers bloom other flowers like roses, but the colour of sandalwood.'

'Do they have any fragrance? Can they be used for puja?' I enquired, unable to restrain my curiosity.

'They have no fragrance, but they are very beautiful to look at. They won't fade if we keep them in a vase.'

Strange! I didn't know what this was. I never saw such flowers. Better to plant sannajaji, so we will have a lot of sweet-smelling flowers. Young girls can deck their plaits with them. The flowers are a nice gift to give women visitors. But why should these flowering plants we have never seen or heard of be grown at all? If we planted the ash-gourd seed instead, and allowed the plant to creep on to the terrace, it would give us many fruits. There would be enough to give away to friends and neighbours too. With just such an idea, I had planted some seeds beside the wall sometime back. They sprouted beautifully too. But a few days later there was no trace of them. I asked both my son and daughter-in-law, 'What happened to the plants here?' They said they didn't know. They must have mistaken the plants for weeds and pulled them out. Of late, my word has about as much value as a blade of grass.

When I suggested that a few brinjals or lady's fingers should be grown, they planted useless cacti and crotons in the same place. They are both alike. They support each other only when I give them some advice. Other times they quarrel over trifles.

I kept quiet as if it didn't concern me. In ten days that seed sprouted. My daughter-in-law's joy knew no bounds. She watched it grow every day, as if it was a very precious thing. As soon as it grew tall enough, she tied it to the pipe on the wall and let the creeper spread all over the terrace. In three months, the creeper spread over the balcony wall. It began to envelop the grille around the balcony. I was very agitated that I might not be able to see the passers-by in the street from the balcony. That was the only way for me to spend time. So I told my daughter-in-law once. I don't know what she thought, but she tied up the creeper tightly with strings and wires so that most of it would creep only on the terrace.

There is only one room upstairs. The rest of it is open terrace. My son uses the room as his study when he returns from office. He spends Sundays with his friends in that room. One day he called his wife and scolded her. I couldn't make out what the quarrel was about. I didn't interfere as it wouldn't have been right.

When my daughter-in-law was cleaning up the house one day, she arranged some flowers in a glass vase in the living-room. Besides yellow and red roses, she put in some shoots with roses the colour of sandalwood. They were strangely attractive. So I held them in my hand and looked at them closely. They looked very dry and brittle.

I asked, 'What kind of flowers are these? They look strange. Why did you put them into the vase with the fresh roses?'

'These are what we call woodroses. In this arrangement, I wanted to show age and youth together. The woodrose stands for old age, the fresh roses symbolise youth. A flower-arrangement like this is called ikebana.'

'Why not call it mother-in-law and daughter-in-law?' I said, smiling. My daughter-in-law also smiled.

From then on, I spent my time in the balcony eagerly watching for the woodroses instead of watching passers-by. I felt some affinity with that plant growing in me. The entire creeper was dotted with pretty, bell-shaped, yellow blossoms. I was waiting for the woodrose to bloom.

One Sunday, when I had finished my puja but it was not yet time for lunch, I went to the balcony to sit there and while away my time.

Then I shouted, 'Why are you pulling out that creeper?'

My son, Gopalam, didn't pay any attention to my question. I saw him cutting down and pulling out the woodrose plant which had spread thickly up to the terrace wall. As he didn't say anything, I went to the kitchen and asked my daughter-in-law, 'Why is he cutting the woodrose plant that way? Come and see.'

'Would he listen to me?' she muttered. 'He can pull out the plant if he wants to. He may pull down the house. Let him ruin it.'

I was worried. So I went to the balcony again and told him it wasn't good to pull out a creeper in full bloom. He shouted at me then. I moved away quietly.

How affectionate he was as a boy! He couldn't bear even a casual remark against me from his father. When the firewood didn't burn and the kitchen was filled with uncomfortable smoke, he would say, 'Amma, when I grow up, I'll see that you don't have the trouble of cooking.' I was deeply touched by these words and tears would well up in my eyes.

He has grown up. I don't have to cook now. My daughter-in-law won't let me step into the kitchen. Should I rejoice at this? After his return from America where he spent three years, he is not able to enjoy spicy food. I use a lot of chillies when I cook. Because I am used to it, I cannot use less chillies. Unlike my daughter-in-law, I cannot cook insipid food. Both of them lecture me that chillies and tamarind are bad for the health. The sweets and other delicacies I used to make have become old-fashioned now. I cannot cook biryani or bake cakes. Even the red-gram chutney is made in the mixie! The old stone-grinder is resting in a corner, useless like me.

As are the adults, so are the children. How can my grandson and granddaughter like my gossip? They spend all their time reading comics. I never heard of these books before. Both of them wear thick glasses already.

When they were eating that night, I stood near their dining-table and asked, 'Gopalam, why did you pull out that plant that way?'

'Which plant?' he asked. Had he forgotten about it already?

'That one, the woodrose plant,' I replied.

'Oh, that! It had become a nuisance. It had covered up the verandah grille and was blocking the light into the hall. It had spread all over the window of the room upstairs, it might have crept all over the terrace. It seemed ready to cover up the whole house. So I pulled it out,' he said carelessly.

'But there were many lovely yellow flowers all over the creeper,' I told him.

'Yes, flowers, and lots of mosquitoes too,' he replied, making a face as if all those mosquitoes bit him at the same time.

I didn't know what else to say.

I went away and lay on my bed. No sleep. A stream of thoughts. The woodrose plant filled my mind. Somehow I felt a lot of pity for it. Who knows, tomorrow my own situation might be the same. The mere thought of it scared me no end.

Maybe the affection between two people should not grow as thick as that dense creeper. If it grows, the youngsters may cut it off and throw it away. The mother only knows how to cling and entwine all round the other.

Translated by E. Nageswara Rao

KUWAIT SAVITRAMMA

CHAKRAVENU

What a bellyful she has fed us, our Savitramma, laddus and khara and all sorts of sweets, nothing lacking at all. She didn't forget the working folk did she? Tell me, is there a single rich farmer around here who has given us a wedding feast like this? We squat outside the wedding house from dawn to dusk and when it's all over they scrape the bottom of the pot to give us a little burnt rice and some thin curry. Has anyone ever given us a good meal with sweetmeats like our Savitramma!' And so the women in the malapalli* spoke, praising Savitramma again and again.

Savitramma was called Kuwait Savitramma by everyone in her village. Kuwait became her family name because she was the first among them to go there to earn some money.

If only my husband were here now, how happy he would be to see his son and daughter married with such pomp . . . How foolish of me, if he were here why should I have gone to Kuwait? For better or worse I would have stayed here with my people, thought Savitramma. She looked at her newly-built house pensively, and the old times spent in the village came back to her. She remembered her husband and wiped her tears with the edge of her sari. Once again she felt the loneliness of life without her husband . . . living in this village where they had lived together . . . in the home they had shared . . . it was impossible. She must return to Kuwait, she decided. But this time she would go alone, without her son. Her visa allowed her to return every year to visit her

---

malapalli: the harijan quarter

son and daughter-in-law, and her daughter and son-in-law. Savitramma sighed at the thought.

Then she drew a deep breath of relief at the thought of having brought her family ashore safely. Now everyone spoke to her with great respect. All of them wanted her help. They wanted visas for their children or sponsorship. 'We won't let this debt remain unpaid, Savitramma,' they said. 'Help us and you will earn punya!' they pleaded.

How these people treated me once! thought Savitramma, as the old memories came back, flooding her mind with those unforgettable experiences.

It was late in the night. Everyone had eaten their evening meal and was ready to go to bed. She heard someone calling at the door and stepped out to see who it was.

'Savitramma! A panchayat has been called outside Big Abba's house and they want you there,' said Dhobi Venkatayya.

'When have I ever come to a hearing, Venkatanna?* If it was a difficult dispute my husband used to go, but after he died who is there in this house to come to a hearing?'

'You haven't been called to hear the dispute, Savitramma! Your people have made a complaint against you. They said go and call her, and so I came, Amma,' explained Venkatayya.

'A complaint against me? Why, have I stabbed someone or destroyed someone's home . . . anyway, who is there Venkatanna?'

'All your relatives, Amma. There is Peddabba's Ramayya, there is your younger brother-in-law Chinnabba. And then there is Sowcar Nagayya. And all the women of your family are there.'

In a flash Savitramma knew why they had called her. But there was no escape . . . what had to happen would happen.

'All right, you go ahead. My mother has gone to the Komti's* house for some areca nuts. The children are asleep at home. As soon as she gets back, I'll be there.'

---

anna: elder brother (used here as a mark of respect)
Komti: a trading community

'I'll wait till your mother comes, it is very late,' said Venkatayya reassuringly. 'How will you come alone?'

When her mother Rajamma returned and heard of the dispute, she was troubled. Her husband too had received many complaints; the relatives seemed bent on taking revenge.

Savitramma set out for Peddabba's house. That was the house in which her husband had grown up. Peddabba was her husband's grandfather. Her husband's father had the same name. The family were among the biggest farmers in the village and the name matched their position in the village. Anything that happened in the village — whether a newcomer needed shelter or a panchayat was to be held — needed the attention of the Peddabba family. Even the village came to be known as Pedduru. But the fortune and influence of the family suffered a decline from Grandfather Peddabba's time to the grandson's. Savitramma's husband, Rajayya, dutifully continued to work the fields when his father wanted to start a business. Neither Savitramma nor her husband questioned his wishes. But when the father suddenly died, all his debts landed on Rajayya's shoulders. He had to sell the land to clear them. Unable to bear the contempt of his kinsmen, he sold the rest of the land to his brothers and moved to a house in the lower quarter of the adjoining village. Barely a year after his father's death Rajayya suddenly died of a heart attack. Rajayya's death left Savitramma without any support, completely destitute. The whole thing still seemed like a nightmare.

A small stream separated the lower quarter and the main village. As Savitramma crossed the stream, she saw the entire village gathered under the street light in front of Peddabba's house, waiting for her. Under the trellis of Peddabba's house her brother-in-law Ramayya sat at one end of a cot; and Sowcar Nagayya on the other. In front of them, to the east of the street, under the street lamp, Savitramma's younger brother-in-law Chinnabba and a few others sat on a heap of stones. There were some more towards the north of the street; and to the south some women huddled together, whispering earnestly. Others sat at their doorstep, waiting to watch the fun. When they saw her, all of them stopped talking at once. Savitramma walked up to her sisters-in-law; but when she sat down, they drew away to a distance, leaving her alone. Savitramma felt like the accused in the dock.

Sowcar Nagayya looked at Savitramma through his glasses and said, 'Ore, Chinnabba! Your sister-in-law has come . . .'

But before he could finish, Chinnabba protested, 'Mama, don't use that word again. She stopped being my sister-in-law the day my brother died!' The sound of whispers grew louder all of a sudden.

'How true,' muttered Savitramma to herself. 'If he was alive I'd be sister-in-law, but he is dead. And barely a month after he died, this man threatened me and raped me. How can I be a sister-in-law to him?'

'Even if you don't think of her as your sister-in-law we have to call her that. Anyway she is here. You had something to say, say it now,' said Nagayya, opening the panchayat meeting. When Nagayya held a panchayat, the village would say: The cunning fox is holding a panchayat. So now grew the murmur, 'Go on, give us the foxy verdict.'

'What is it Chinnabba?' said Nagayya.

'Why ask me, Mama?' shouted Chinnabba. 'What she does makes us bow our heads before the village. Everyone is talking about her. She has made our family the laughing-stock of the village. This is something all of you know!'

'Ore, Chinnabba! If you shout, it is our honour that is lost. She has no sense of shame has she?' asked Ramayya, Savitramma's older brother-in-law, in a low drawl. Then he yelled, 'You, Chinnabba! Say what you have to about this woman now. We have to settle this one way or the other today.'

But Chinnabba asked his brother, 'Why me? Why don't you talk?'

'If you split your belly your guts will spill over your feet. So our elders said. Why don't *you* tell us,' said Nagayya gently, reminding Chinnabba of the plan they had made earlier.

'Mama, this woman has committed adultery with so many men. We beat her up, scolded her, but she did not mend her ways. She has brought dishonour to us. Now there is a son of a . . . who has come from far-off

Kuwait. He is from her mother's village, a man called Rahman. She is running around with him, bringing more disgrace to our family!' Chinnabba was bursting with righteous anger as the real issue came out into the open.

'Well, Savitramma, is this the truth?' asked Nagayya.

'What is this? Why do you ask her? If she stays in this village, everyone will point a finger at us and our daughters will not get married!' Ramayya added his voice to strengthen his brother's complaint. 'Either she must leave the village today or we will.'

Tears filled Savitramma's eyes and spilt over as she sat silent. The murmur from the crowd grew louder.

Then Chengavva reassured her, 'Look here Savitramma, why do you bend your head and weep? Are all these women chaste pativratas and are you the lone sinner here? As long as we can hide our sins we are all chaste! Rip off the mask and the truth will come out! What is there to be afraid of? Say what you want to openly.'

'Woman! Can't you hear them? Why are you mute like a dumb bullock?' thundered Nagayya.

'What do you want me to say, Anna? All of you are with those who have power and the loudest voices. Is anyone willing to listen to me and carry out justice?' Savitramma's voice quivered. Then in the gathering silence she slowly began again.

'These people speak as if I've committed some crime. Did any one of them help me after my husband died? Did they think of my children and give me a seer of rice or a rupee to find a meal? You say I have no sense of shame. But how else will I feed my children? Do you think I do it for fun? Or because I am fat and full of lust? Whether I work and earn a living, whether my children and I starve or rot together in our hovel, what is it to anyone here? Now you want to deprive me of that shelter also. So be it. My children and I will leave this village. Let them take my life too and rule like kings!'

A weeping Savitramma turned her back on the crowd and ran home.

She left the next morning with her mother and children by a passenger train. From her mother's village, she left for Kuwait with the help of relatives and Rahman Saab's support. She finally returned to her village as a woman of property. It had been easy to regain her old position and respect. It seemed so strange now as she thought about it.

As she stretched out on the cot in her balcony, the past seemed unbelievable. The very relatives who had driven her out were treating her with such respect! Then she heard footsteps and her name being called out, rousing her from her reverie. She saw her brother-in-law Chinnabba and his wife Ramalakshamma approaching.

'Akka! Why do you sit here weeping when we asked you to come for lunch? You know that a daughter must go to her mother-in-law someday however much you cherish her,' said Ramalakshamma to comfort her. She did not guess that Savitramma's tears were not for her daughter. But Savitramma knew that even in the past Ramalakshamma had not really been against her; she had kept her distance out of fear of her husband.

'Come, Akka, come and eat,' Ramalakshamma pleaded.

'Why, I have cooked some rice here,' replied Savitramma.

All this while Chinnabba stood silent, remembering his role in her past. Savitramma guessed why he was silent, and she too did not speak to him at all.

'Akka, is it true that you are returning to Kuwait this week?'

'Yes, I stayed this long only because of the wedding. I should have gone back long ago. I am taking the Janata Express to Bombay and from there I leave for Kuwait.' Savitramma spoke without a trace of anger.

There was a brief silence. Chinnabba then nudged his wife to remind her of the real purpose of their visit. 'Your brother-in-law also wants to come to Kuwait, Akka,' mumbled Ramalakshamma.

'I didn't bring any visas this time. I was busy with the wedding. I will ask Rahman Mama if he has any and let you know,' said Savitramma.

'Rahman Anna said he had only brought visas for women.'

Savitramma was filled with amazement. This was the same Chinnabba who had threatened to set fire to the house in which she and Rahman Saab were together. And now Rahman Saab was Anna!

'Since you have no visas for men, your brother-in-law wants me to go with you. If you say yes, I'll come, Akka,' said Ramalakshamma hesitantly.

'I have no say in this. If Rahman Mama agrees, come along. But it is a hard life there. Don't come unless you are willing to face it. You can't refuse to do that work after you get there. You will suffer a lot. Better think it over.' Savitramma raised her voice so that her brother-in-law would hear her.

'I'm going to the field for a while,' said Chinnabba promptly and left.

The two women sat together in silence for some time. Then Savit-ramma said, 'I will leave for Kuwait a few days after I get to Bombay. You can't come with me, Ramalakshamma. You will need a medical certificate, a passport and a visa. All this will take at least two to three months.'

'Rahman Mama told my husband the same thing.'

'Did he ask your husband to go with you to Bombay?'

'Rahman Mama told him, Why waste the money, Chinnabba? I will take good care of her.'

Her innocence stirred pity in Savitramma. Obviously her husband hadn't told her the truth. She hadn't understood Rahman's intentions either!

'Look Ramalakshamma, I want to tell you something. You shouldn't feel later that I didn't even warn you. You will be in Bombay for a couple of months. The agents who take you around there won't treat you with any respect. They will send you to several men. This is the hard truth. You will have to obey every order whether you like it or not. Otherwise you can forget about going to Kuwait. Don't think women go to Kuwait so easily. You better think it over carefully.'

Ramalakshamma began to weep. 'My husband knows all this and still he wants me to go. He said I was to agree to everything I was asked to do. When I refused he beat me up. Rather than die of his blows I thought it was better to go . . .'

'I couldn't bear to see my children starve, so I got into this business,' burst out Savitramma, unable to control herself. 'Your husband called

a panchayat and drove me out of the village. What does he call what you
are about to become?'

'You know everything, what can I say to you Akka?'

'Yes, when a lot of money is involved, men like this not only run the
business but also sell their wives!' said Savitramma bitterly. Slowly she
calmed herself. 'I'm leaving on Sunday by the Janata Express. If you
want to come, you will have to book your ticket in advance. I will stay
with you in Bombay for at least ten days and see you through.'

That Sunday evening the platform was packed with people. It was as
if all of Pedduru had come to see Savitramma and Ramalakshamma off!
Every week two or three people left for Kuwait. That day there were
many more. They held their relatives and wept. 'Write as soon as you
arrive and tell us how you are,' they said.

Suddenly there was a commotion; a large group came to the platform,
weeping. All eyes turned to them. It was a young Muslim girl, barely
seventeen, unmarried. She wept in such terror that her wails seemed to
rise to the sky and spread in every direction.

'Don't worry my child, Mama is with you. He will look after you.
Just bear it for two years and then you can come back. We will get you
married,' the mother comforted her daughter.

'How terrible!' said the onlookers. 'How can they send away an
unmarried girl? Isn't it better to beg here for a few grains?'

'This is like sending a lamb to the slaughter-house. Are those parents
human beings?'

As the train drew into the station people jostled each other and ran
towards the compartments. Savitramma sank into her seat. Her son and
daughter-in-law, daughter and son-in-law and other relatives said good-
bye.

Ramalakshamma wept piteously as she held her relatives. Chinnabba
wore a look of suffering as if he could not bear to be parted from his
wife. Some of the elders comforted him as the train began to move.

Rahman Saab pulled Ramalakshamma into the compartment. The
sound of weeping from the platform rose, so loud that it drowned out

the sound of the train. People stood there, waving till the train disappeared from view.

Ramalakshamma's sorrow drew sympathetic looks from fellow-travellers. She was leaving her village, her people and her parents behind. She was broken with grief.

Savitramma was neither surprised nor disturbed by this grief. It was such a routine thing now. Her tears no longer spilt over. But her heart was heavy as she leaned back in her seat.

Translated by Vasantha Kannabiran

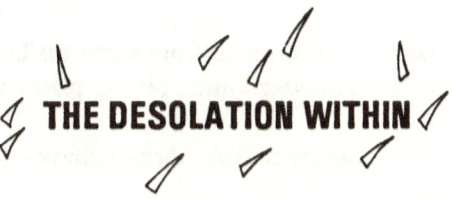

THE DESOLATION WITHIN

ALLAM RAJAIAH

It is a small railway station, built in the days of the Niz·m of Hyderabad. The plaster on the station building has peeled off in this year's heavy rains. Rainwater draining down the roof has left dark smudges on the walls. The fencing built with cement poles on either side of the building is broken in places. Passengers coming in and out pass through the broken fence more often than through the main door of the station.

There are some living quarters behind, built along with the station, four of which are in a dilapidated state. The railway gangmen live in the rest of them, not the stationmaster or the booking clerk. They stay in a smallish town twenty kilometres away and travel up and down every day.

To the south of the station there are some eucalyptus trees. The ground underneath is bright with fallen leaves. Across the station are neem and babul trees, and green shrubs. Under the trees, on the other side of the track, sit four gloomy-looking toddy-tappers with their

TRANSLATOR'S NOTE: The story takes place in a wayside railway station, apparently to the south of Peddapalli in Karimnagar district. On the south-bound trunk route from Delhi, nameless long-distance express trains roar past, but there is also a smaller universe of local trains that connect the mining towns of the Singareni Collieries Company in the north, to Hyderabad and Warangal in the south, via Kazipet junction. The queen of this universe is the Singareni Express, which brings the dead boy's father, Rajaram. The railway policeman in the story describes the villages around as 'dangerous areas;' that is, the area has an active naxalite presence. This presence is obliquely referred to at various points in the story, and perhaps the final invocation is addressed to them. The story is written in the distinctive rural idiom of North Telengana, not easily reproduced in conventional or literary English.

foaming toddy pots. At some distance from them sits Upendram of the effeminate mouth, his yellow-coloured plastic plate piled high with liquor packets.*

Sheikh Dawood's mirchis, fried that morning, have become stale; and that makes him grumble.

The three peasant women selling roasted cobs of maize under the neem tree hurl abuses at each other.

And the old woman who sells wild berries has an unfathomable look of dejection.

Over there, a family waits with an uncertain air about them; they cannot sit in the dust under the trees, nor can they stand for long. 'Why don't you go find out when that wretched train is coming,' the wife says impatiently to the husband. Her name is Gangamma; she is dressed in a pink polyester sari, and wears gold earrings, silver toe-rings and anklets.

Her husband Rajesam dips his fingers into the pocket of his shirt and gives her a meaningful smile. He wears a dhoti and a white polyester shirt. He has a muffler around his neck, and a watch on his left wrist.

'Amma, I want those berries,' whines their ten-year-old son.

'Ask your father,' says Gangamma curtly.

Since his wife did not object to his smile, Rajesam walks up to Upendram and asks, 'How much for a packet, boy?'

'How much do they charge in your collieries?' asks Upendram.

'Do you sell at the same rate?'

'If we sell at the same rate as the coal mines, won't they break our bones?' asks a toddy-tapper angrily.

'Who's they?' asks Rajaram.

'Who else? They who can pull out the serpent's fangs,' says a second toddy-tapper.

Rajesam does not ask who can pull out a serpent's fangs.

'Two-fifty a packet,' says Upendram.

The country liquor or arrack drunk by the working classes was, till recently, sold by the government in polythene packets. The sole selling rights were auctioned area-wise, and the contractor who bought the rights employed people like Upendram to sell the packets.

'Quite cheap,' says someone. 'In our village it was four rupees when the contract was new, but after the rumpus it has come down.'

'Not just your village — it is the same rate in all the villages here. Believe me, the fellow who bid for the contract in our village this year has gone to the dogs.'

'At our collieries it is sheer robbery. They charge five rupees,' says Rajesam. He takes two packets, puts one in his pocket, bites into the other and has a drink. He takes out a five-rupee note and pays for them.

A teacher by his side shifts uneasily, as if the stench has gone straight into her nostrils.

An old woman with dangling earrings asks her grandson, 'When will the train come, my son? After it is quite dark?' Her trousered grandson, sitting on a bag of rice, says, 'It's a passenger train, you can't know till the bell goes.'

At a distance, a totally drunk farmer who has evidently seen better days is cursing somebody vehemently.

'They have crucified you, my son o' Christ, they have nailed each limb, my son o' Christ,' sings an old man with an amputated leg — it was run over by a train. He sings like one who has personally seen the crucifixion. The tremor in his voice brings tears to the listeners' eyes. He stumps around among the people with his hand outstretched.

Rajesam, moving on to find out when the train is coming, drops a twenty-five paise coin in his palm and says, 'It is the poor, not Christ that they have crucified.'

Suddenly an express train rushes past behind him with an ear-splitting roar. Rajesam waits till it passes, then crosses the tracks. His son, who has followed him, is scared; he runs back to his mother.

Inside the station, the ticket-booking window is closed. Rajesam peeps into the stationmaster's room. He sees the stationmaster, sitting at an old table, looking even older. He has a worried look on his face. A railway policeman rushes in, removes his cap, and mops his head.

'It was a donkey's job getting all the details about that fellow, sir,' he says, all the pains he has taken showing on his face. 'It seems, sir, about a week ago he was found in this station, shivering in the cold, and was taken to the police station. You know this is a dangerous area! Moreover he's a young fellow, and he would not answer any of their questions. It seems they thrashed him from morning till evening but he would not talk. He finally told them about his mother. Enquiries were made and it was learnt that his people originally belonged to Ramulapalli. His father is a tramp. He has sold away their lands and is loafing around Peddapalli. He's an old hand — spent one year at Karimnagar sub-jail. It was the boy's mother who worked to bring him up . . . finally they decided he was a vagrant and let him off.' The railway policeman stops to take a breath.

'Whatever he was, this is a big nuisance for us. We'll have to shiver in the cold all night once the passenger train is off,' says the stationmaster.

'But sir, suppose we pretend it is an unknown vagrant and finish the inquest . . .'

'These are evil days,' demurs the stationmaster. 'Suppose we get into trouble! You stand watch near the corpse. Rangaiah will get some tea. Meanwhile I'll try to get hold of his mother and father.'

'What is it?' Rajesam asks the railway policeman coming out of the room.

'What else can it be — murder, homicide, to kill and get killed — in today's world you kill yourself or you kill somebody.'

'Okay, don't tell me if you don't want to. You don't have to go on like that just because I asked you a question,' says Rajesam.

'I have strained my jaw repeating the story again and again since the morning. Near that cabin over there some son of a whore put his head under a train. I told the stationmaster we'll get rid of the inquest, but the very idea makes him wet his pants. His father must have been a bigger vagrant than this fellow!' The railway policeman tugs again and again at the wet uniform that clings to his skin in the heat.

Meanwhile, the stationmaster rings up Peddapalli.

'The police station here has already got a wireless message. The police have got hold of the father. He is being brought by the Singareni Express,' says a voice from the other side.

He then rings up the mother's village. Fortunately there is a railway station there. 'The mother and some relatives are coming in a bullock cart,' is the reply.

The stationmaster comes out of his room to tell the railway policeman who stands guard over the corpse.

'Sir, when is the passenger train coming?' asks Rajesam.

'Don't bother me,' says the stationmaster, irritated, his eyes searching for the gangmen.

'I am going to look at the corpse sir,' says Rajesam. 'What shall I tell them?'

'Tell them his father is coming by the Singareni.'

Seeing Rajesam walk swiftly toward the cabin, his arms swinging by his side, Gangamma shouts from the other side of the track, 'Is it time for the train? Where the devil are you off to?'

Rajesam ignores her and walks fast. The sand crackles under his boots.

Midway between the cabin and the platform, about a hundred yards to the cabin, there is a cluster of people.

There are four people with bags in their hands, a look of commiseration on their faces.

The railway policemen, oblivious of the corpse, sit smoking beedis and exchanging gossip.

To one side of the Delhi track there is a headless body reclining on a heap of stones. A piece of white cloth barely covers it. The head lies on the track; its eyes are terrifyingly wide-open. Between the head and the trunk is a pool of blood swarming with huge flies.

The face is still tender. It has barely started to grow a moustache. The jawbones are prominent. What a beautiful face! The hair on the head is clotted with blood. Since the cloth covering the body is not long enough, the feet and calves show. The ankles are lacerated; he must have been really thrashed. The trousers are torn.

Rajesam sobers down quickly. He feels a hand churning his stomach. 'There is nothing more sinful than a human birth,' he spits.

In his mind he sees the dead bodies of his fellow mine-workers, crushed under a fallen roof.

Rajesam squats and weeps, 'O son! What a fate you have sought, you who are yet to know pain and pleasure.'

'What does fate have to do with it?' says a policeman called Rangaiah. 'When the time comes to die nobody can escape it.'

'Go away . . .' yells another railway policeman, trying to drive away the people who have gathered around.

'How much he must have suffered to be driven to this . . .' says a young farmer's son. He is on his way to compete in a running race to get a job with the Singareni mining company.

An old man intones, 'To be undaunted by trouble, and to come out unscathed like Sita from the ordeal of fire, is the mark of a real human being.'

'Troubles — so what! Trouble is as natural as pleasure. That's human life. But today's youth want all the good things to drop at their feet,' says Rangaiah.

'True, dora* — if only everyone got a job like you,' says an old woman.

'So what if you do not get a job? Does that mean you kill yourself?' argues Rangaiah.

'What else can one do? Beg for food? Or rob others?' asks someone from the crowd.

'Either way it means trouble,' adds the young man.

One of the railway policemen throws away his beedi butt and agrees, 'True . . .'

'The fellow who has guts will not die, he will kill others,' says Rangaiah; this is a truth he has distilled from experience. He walks towards the station.

'Which train did he fall under, son?' asks the old woman.

Rajesam feels faint. Rage contorts his face, a rage such as the miners feel when one of them dies in the collieries. He recalls the railway policeman's words to the stationmaster: A week ago the police took him away on a charge of vagrancy. Rajesam says in an angry voice, 'There is nothing more wretched than a human birth. The honest and artless

---

dora: my lord

cannot survive in this accursed world. Who knows why the young fellow left home? Maybe he had a fight, maybe his feelings were hurt. The father who ought to teach good and bad is supposed to have lost his own bearings and become a vagrant; and what can the mother, a woman, do? She must have suffered, and the boy too must have suffered, for her and for the father who had gone nobody knows where . . . Who knows how much the boy suffered? Maybe if somebody had drawn him close and healed the pain in his heart, maybe he would have survived. But the police would not have thought of that. They just thrashed the boy who was all raw inside. Is this . . .'

'It's none of your business, my hero,' says one of the policemen. 'If you talk any more I'll hand you over to the police station.'

Rajesam pulls out a packet from his pocket, bites into it and takes a drink. He challenges him, 'Come on, hand me over, let us see you do it.'

'What do you think you can do — why don't you just look on like the others? Why do you talk so much — are you the dead fellow's brother or brother-in-law?' asks the policeman.

'I am more than that,' says Rajesam and lunges at the policeman.

The by-standers separate them. Rajesam's wife Gangamma sees all this from afar and comes running across the tracks. She is struck dumb at the sight of the corpse. She stops cursing and takes her husband by the arm and drags him away.

For a while Rajesam sits on the bag of rice with his head in his hands. A scene flits across his mind — a group of miners standing by dead bodies in the collieries, shouting angrily. He suddenly gets up and buys two more packets of liquor. Gangamma is busy describing what she has seen and ignores him.

Those who have already seen the corpse are adding details. Those who have not walk over to take a look.

It is close to five in the evening. The winter's day is drawing to a close. The western sky is like a forest on fire. The sun has the flushed look of a child that has wept itself faint. The shade of the neem and babul trees, and the shrubs on the other side of the station, has spread over the whole area. The cold seeps through the air like melancholy.

More and more people arrive at the station. They are from neighbouring villages — mostly workers from the collieries or their relations. Only a few people go to Kazipet from that station, and most of these are railway workers working on the recent track electrification.

All the newcomers take a look at the corpse. There is a withdrawn look on their faces. The hawkers of toddy and country liquor are doing brisk business. The dead body has raised a tempest in each heart. It is as if they are trying to quench it.

Sheikh Dawood's mirchis have sold out.

Their talk is a perambulation around life and death.

An old worker who lives in the quarters has just come home from duty. He has bathed and is going about the station in a dhoti. 'That boy was roaming about the station ten days back,' he says. 'He would not speak to anyone. He would sit with a lost look on his face. Once in a while he would run here and there, shouting like someone demented. A couple of days back we found him in a swoon and gave him some food. Someone told his mother he was here and she came to fetch him. That's the last I saw of him.'

All of them seem to know this story. They look as if they too have run here and there with burning hearts. Something is eating away at their insides. It seems to unravel itself little by little, but then suddenly it becomes entangled. Something is boiling over in the cauldron of these villages. All human feeling, all ties — home, children, land, crops, weddings, the sun and the rain — all, all are breaking up. The strongest tie of all, their attachment to land, is cut; they are leaving the villages, the umbilical cord sundered, roaming about in search of a livelihood.

They grumble. Strange new words crackle like a funeral pyre. Their crumbled wisdom makes a meaningless commotion in the station.

A railway worker in shorts beats the iron gong to announce a train. Strange — he beats it with his teeth clenched, like one possessed!

The people run to the booking window. The sleepy booking-clerk gives out tickets slowly, without looking at their eager faces.

'How late is the passenger train, dora,' asks Rajesam, with an attempt at drunken familiarity. The clerk seems immune; he does not reply.

'To Ramagundam — two full and two halves,' says Rajesam.

By the time he is on the platform, those waiting for the Singareni Express are restless. Soon that train pulls in noisily. Some get off the train. Fewer still get into the train which leaves for Kazipet.

One of those who have got off the train is a tall, middle-aged man. He has a narrow face and discoloured teeth. The hair on his head is dirty. His polyester shirt is torn at the shoulders. The dhoti is made of fine material but is worn out. His feet are bare and the legs dirty till the knees. His ankles are cracked, like a parched paddy field. His bones are visible through his skin. He looks like a skeleton six feet tall. The face has a beaten look. And the eyes — nobody there is able to make out those eyes. In a word he looks like the captain of a vanquished army. In his hand he has a worn-out businessman's bag, torn at the corners. In the other hand he has two Telugu newspapers. They are so stained it is difficult to make out how old they are.

A dark and well-built railway policeman gets off the train with him. He is bent, and his face is like coal crushed in the seams of the earth.

The railway policeman takes the tall man into the stationmaster's room. The news soon spreads: The father of the boy who fell under the train has come! People move towards the stationmaster's room to take a look at him.

'You have finally come,' says the stationmaster, putting on his coat.

The tall man is not weeping as a father would. He does not run to look at his blood that has congealed in the corpse. It is as if he has already been through all this. He sits in the chair across the stationmaster's, as if to say, What is the hurry?

The people looking in from the windows and the door are at first surprised. Then they whisper among themselves, 'The man is a lump of stone!'

'Look, he is not even sweating!'

'There is no affection in him.'

The tall man turns his head and looks back at them. He seems to see a lot of half-burnt faces. He seems to smell the burning of human flesh all over the place.

'Let's get going, Rajaram,' says the railway policeman wearily.

'Where to?' asks the tall man whose name is now revealed.

'What do you mean, where to? Are you here for my son's wedding? I had a donkey's time searching all over Peddapalli for you,' bursts out the railway policeman.

'So what do you want me to do?'

'Won't you take a look at your deceased son?' asks the stationmaster.

Rajaram looks at the stationmaster's face as if it is his son's. 'What is there to look at?' he asks.

'This son of a whore will be the end of the world!' The stationmaster nearly loses his head. He has seen many a death in the course of doing his job; some animals and some human beings. If it is a human death, the station usually resounds to the clamour of weeping. People rush pell-mell to the corpse. It is always a tough job to calm them and get the inquest completed. But look at this fellow. He is not even thinking of the death. Is this a man or an animal? Or a lump of rock? Is this fellow really the dead boy's father?

Meanwhile, Rajaram rubs his face.

'Listen, how long do you think we can keep the corpse here — he died at four-thirty in the morning. The corpse is already smelling. The inquest has to be completed,' reasons the stationmaster.

'Complete it, then,' says Rajaram.

'Let us go there.'

'And?'

'You look at your son and laugh and we will weep,' bursts out the policeman.

Rajaram looks at the policeman's face. He sees the roots of a burnt-out mahua tree.

Rajaram stands up, apparently impatient with these arguments. He has, in fact, seen his son's dead body long ago in his mind. The strange thought suddenly strikes him: When did his son's death begin? He had always believed that a person does not die in an instant. Death happens over many years.

Even after the stationmaster and the railway policeman have left the room, Rajaram stands rooted to the spot, wondering when exactly his son had started dying.

'Hey, Rajaram!' the policeman calls. Rajaram walks out of the room like a man in a dream. The people outside surround him.

'What a sinful man,' an old woman mutters.

'You look like a man of some education — don't you know that young people these days don't like being abused? What did you do to him? Did you scold him or beat him?'

'Is there no sense in your head?'

The abuse and the benediction — and some advice on child-rearing — leaves Rajaram unmoved. He looks around as if trying to find out at what moment each of them had begun to die. He also searches to see if there is one among them who has conquered death.

Rajesam slides up to Rajaram and asks in an affectionate tone, 'How many children did you have?'

'Only one,' answers Rajaram.

Some of the people get even more angry. 'You brute! What sort of a man are you? You can't even look after one son!' an old man abuses him.

'Chah! Are there such sinful people in this world who can't care for their own sons and daughters?' asks another, this one a middle-aged man.

'Well, here is one for you . . .'

'Which of us can guarantee his own well-being these days! We all think we will live well. But fate may decree otherwise — this boy's fate was written thus by the Creator,' says another.

'It is men who decree our fate . . .' says Rajesam.

Rajaram walks in silence.

The crowd follows him; the policeman and stationmaster lead.

Dusk has descended. The west is a mixture of black and red, like a cold and burnt-out village on the horizon.

Rajaram stops at a water pump. Someone pumps water. He washes his face and takes a drink. Seeing him search his pockets, someone offers a packet of beedis and matches. Someone else also offers cigarettes but he refuses. He takes a beedi and returns the packet, but the man refuses to take it back.

Rajaram walks on, puffing at the beedi.

A mob has already gathered at the corpse.

Rajaram looks at his flesh and blood lying by the railway track.

The people around look at Rajaram's face and the corpse's face in turn. They have the same features, and strangely — the same look.

Rajaram stands as immobile as a stone.

At a glance from the stationmaster, a railway policeman removes the cloth covering the body.

Rajaram drops feebly at the corpse's feet.

'What an unfeeling heart you have,' someone says.

Words such as 'a stone' and 'a sinful man' are heard. And the piteous remark, 'At such a virile age . . .'

Rajaram is impervious to these remarks. His mind is invaded by images. Crumbled huts, tiled roofs that have caved in, grain scattered on the floor, broken mud vessels: the image of a devastated village fills his head.

Rajaram looks like a desolate village. Like a forest consumed and left cold, burnt-out, by a wild fire. Like a river run dry, like a lake parched, the mud underneath cracked, he sits silent.

Like a plough-bullock with an empty stomach that wanders from house to house in a destroyed village, he loiters among the broken pieces of his forgotten past. The broken pieces move strangely, very strangely, in his mind. It seems to him that his son's death began long before he was born to him.

A half-naked boy runs behind his father. The peasant strides on with a shovel in one hand and a bucket to draw water slung over his shoulder. The boy's feet are smarting with the heat. The father gathers the boy in his arms, cursing him. The boy is intrigued by the fibrous hair that sprouts on maize. 'Ayya, do the cobs grow moustaches?' he asks.

Somebody is wailing in the desolate village. The father's body, with the fair, crumpled skin and a blue stone in the earring, is laid out in front of the house. Amma flings herself on the body and wails. She wails till it seems she will tear her intestines . . . Then the eldest brother, with hair stiff as bamboo, a clerk with the village patel; the sister-in-law tall and loud of voice . . . The brother drinks himself to death. The home is broken . . . The boy moves from schoolroom to plough . . . He cannot remember which of them died first, his father or his brother.

By the time he takes up the plough there are only ten acres of land. And there is a loan from the Cooperative Bank to get a well dug . . . The loan is never repaid. A fresh loan is taken from the new Land Mortgage Bank to get a motor for the well . . . The crop of chillies is attacked by a pest and all their labour is wasted . . . The bankers take away the big cart. In the midst of these confused memories floats up the image of a woman with flushed cheeks.

Drink, daily fisticuffs and kicking . . . By that time he is reduced to aimless wandering, like a machine gone out of control. His wife hires out her labour for weeding and transplanting. She moves out of the death-trap and takes their son with her. Rajaram has not seen her since then. He would drink, and he would tend the crops of his landlord. He would work for one month and loaf around for two. He would roam wherever his fancy took him. And then the party* came to these villages . . . By the time that trouble began, he had become a tendu* contractor. He had paid the labourers the rate the naxalites decided, and for that the police had taken him away. He could remember nothing much afterwards. He had offered his old house as security to bail out a village youth who had been arrested. The young man disappeared after he was released, and Rajaram couldn't make good the security money. He was jailed for six months. Later, the house was attached. He could remember little of where he had gone, or what he had done afterwards. His memory goes blank then.

---

party: here a reference to the naxalites
tendu: the tendu leaf, used to roll beedis, is abundant in the forests of North Telengana. The poor and landless peasants pick the leaf and sell it to the 'contractor,' who sells it to the beedi-making companies after paying the government its fee.

The railway policemen bring the head into position near the body. One of them is writing the inquest report. Another is driving away the onlookers.

'When did he leave home?' asks the stationmaster.

'Whose home?' Rajaram wakes up.

'Yours, of course.'

Rajaram is silent. He looks again and again from the dead body of his son, now with its head in position, to the people gathered around. Is that really his son? How sweet the four-year-old face was! How many questions there were in his heart! With what avidity the tiny eyes would drink in the trees, the animals, the birds he saw! There are no questions at all in this face. When exactly was it destroyed?

'Don't you have a home at all?' The stationmaster is angry.

'No,' says Rajaram, as if he resents the intrusion of these questions just when his memories are piecing together.

'When did he run away?'

'Who?'

'Your son, of course!'

Rajaram does not answer. He is not even able to remember the first question.

'When exactly did your son leave home?' the stationmaster asks again.

The people around are impatient. 'The poor fellow has lost his wits,' says someone in the crowd.

'Give him a packet of liquor and it will come back,' suggests a man standing by Rajaram.

Rajesam runs to get two packets. But Rajaram looks at them as if he has never seen liquor before and refuses the offer . . . He seems to be in a stupor stronger than that of alcohol. He was quite sober when he came to the station. There were no thoughts, no memories. But now thoughts spin in his head.

'How old is your son?' the stationmaster asks. He asks the question just when Rajaram is suddenly struck by a desire to touch the body.

'I do not know . . .' There is a hard note in Rajaram's reply.

Just then they hear a woman's voice wailing, and an emaciated woman comes running towards the corpse, crying and beating her breast. An old man walks behind her with the help of a stick; and two peasants like lean plough-bullocks.

. The woman looks even poorer than Rajaram, and prematurely aged. She wears a patchwork of two differently coloured saris. It is torn here and there, and her choli is faded with use. Her hair is dishevelled. And there is not an ounce of flesh on her bony face.

'O koduka! Oh my son! What a thing you have taken upon yourself! Did I not feed you with my own hands only the evening before yesterday? Your mother has come, my son! Your thatha has come, Malliah! Your uncles have come. What is your farewell to this destitute mother? I bore you but I could not bear your fate! Devuda, may ruin overtake your temple! You have thrown my life to the dogs, O God! My father gave me no happiness. Mine is a sinful life. Nor did the one I married give me any happiness, O God! The sun has set over the forest, my son. What more should I live for? Why did you not take me with you?' The woman weeps as if demented, caressing the body; every now and then she heaps dust from the ground on her head.

Till this moment all the hearts there were frozen, but now they melt. 'A mother's womb . . . a woman's heart cannot help breaking . . . it is the child from her own womb that lies dead,' says an old woman, weeping freely.

Tears engulf all of them, like the cold, like the darkness. The railway policeman writing the inquest report forgets what he has been doing. The stationmaster wipes his glasses.

Rajaram hears the weeping as if from a distance. Is that wailing woman his wife? Did he share a life with that woman once upon a time? Did he share the afternoon meals with her, working in the maize field? No, this is not that woman. Rajaram remembers only a smiling woman, with her bright face and flushed cheeks. This woman looks like a demon.

The old man with the walking-stick slumps to the ground. 'Quiet, Yellamma. You will weep your eyeballs out. Nobody can escape fate.

No one is here forever,' he says.

She falls into her father's arms and weeps, 'O Ayya, give courage to your grandson, wake him up, Ayya.' The old man hugs his daughter with his frail arms. His hands shake.

It's a long time before Yellamma becomes quiet. She then sees the man sitting at her son's feet. She shrinks as if she has seen a ghost.

'Go away — don't touch my son. He will be infected by your poison. You who destroyed my life. It is you who killed my son,' she shouts. And she pulls her son's legs towards her.

Somebody takes Rajaram away. Yellamma again falls on her son's body and cries, 'Your father never came to see how you lived, koduka! Now he has come to see you die! Come, ask him all the questions you used to ask me, Malliah my son!'

The railway policeman comes to his senses. He tries to come up with some consoling wisdom, but he can think of nothing to say.

Rajaram is troubled by several questions. Would his son not have died if he had lived with him? But how could he live with them when he was himself dead? When had his own death begun, who had destroyed his dreams, and when? When and where had his tears dried up? Was he a lump of hard rock? Who had snapped each of his nerves, one by one? His dead brother? Had it happened the day he left school and became the mainstay of a large family? Or the day the crop of chillies was killed by a pest? Or the day the sahukar took away his land? Or the day the Land Mortgage Bank held the auction? Or the day the pauperized farmer became a day labourer? No, not any one of these events; each of them had snapped one after the other of his life's nerves.

He too had wept like this that day, after his brother's death, when he had left the eighth-standard classroom and gone to work with his father, and his calloused hands were stained with dried blood; and again the day his father died; when the burden of the family fell on his shoulders he had slumped under the banyan tree and wept thus. He had later sold his land acre by acre; he had writhed as if he was being chopped up limb by limb. The day all the land was sold he had withered like a tree whose roots have been cut. His tears had dried up then.

This devastation had taken place in every village, in the heart of every farmer. They go around with their wounds hidden, the desolation secreted in the heart. They go around like leaves driven before a blowing wind.

The railway policeman brings the completed report. Rajaram puts his signature on it in English.

The corpse is taken away. The people move with it. It is taken out of the station covered with a cloth, to the accompaniment of consoling words. Yellamma follows the corpse, leaning on her old father, beating her breast and weeping.

Rajaram too comes out of the station with the others.

Paddy straw is laid out on the cart and smoothened. The body is stretched out on it. Yellamma sits in the cart, the dead boy's head in her lap, showering kisses on it like a mad woman.

In the light of the street lamp outside the station, the gathering looks like a procession of ghosts.

'Did I not love people, land, my crops? My wife, son, father, family . . .' Rajaram feels something engulf him; he feels the beginning of a slight tremor.

He feels a sudden desire to take his son's head in his arms and kiss him. The four-year-old child sits on his shoulder, pestering him with questions.

'Get into the cart, my bava.' His wife's brother who is driving the cart invites Rajaram.

'Who is this bava you are inviting? My life is in ashes . . . your bava has long been dead and I am a sinful widow. Drive on . . .' says Yellamma.

The cart moves on.

The gong is struck in the railway station. It is time for the passenger train. People, shaken out of their absorption, run noisily on to the platform.

Rajaram stands alone outside the station, not knowing which way to go. His feet move in the direction of the cart.

The station is soon left behind. In the dark he can hear the creaking of the cart, the sound of gravel crunching under its wheels. The surrounding darkness is flooded by the nameless humming of some insect. Bright, phosphorescent glow-worms fly above the date palms. The stars shine overhead. The distant lights of villages are like the torches of ghosts . . . The cart has moved ahead. He can no longer hear it creaking.

Left behind, his feet come to a halt. He slumps on to the ground.

'Are you coming, my bava?' shouts his wife's brother.

Rajaram does not shout back. He is not strong enough.

Does his brother-in-law really expect him to come? Is he going to attend his son's funeral? Is he truly the father of the boy who fell under the train this morning? In these burnt and desolate villages, who is father and who is son?

The cold is more intense. And the pangs of hunger add to it. His jaws tremble, and he suddenly remembers the liquor packets. Something hard and resilient in him, that will not accept this logic, has begun to melt. It hurts him more than both cold and hunger. He has a splitting pain in the head.

He feels an urge to cry out loud, loud enough to be heard wherever the earth was born. But he is not able to weep. How much more fortunate is the mother who has gone in that cart!

He stands up. Unsteadily, he begins to walk, neither toward the station, nor forward in the direction of the cart, but to the east. There is no proper path here. He walks across shrubs and creepers till he finally finds a cart-track. He walks on and reaches a banyan tree. It is the tree of the goddess Pochamma. One track from this tree goes to Rajaram's village. One goes to Peddapalli. The third goes across ploughed fields to the Ramagiri forests, and the fourth goes to a neighbouring village.

The desolate son of a farmer slumps down under the tree, his mind blank, rubbing his head and face with his hands. Rajaram, son of a farmer, weeps uncontrollably. Weeping, he melts little by little and seeps into the earth.

Rajaram weeps at the crossroads, in the cold, in the dark, in hunger, in grief for the son he has lost and for all that was his, and that he has lost.

From which of the four paths will they come — the wayfarers who will understand the desolation within Rajaram, then arouse him and fold him in their arms?

Translated by K. Balagopal

NOTES ON CONTRIBUTORS

ABBURI CHAYA DEVI worked as a librarian for more than two decades in the United States Information Service, Delhi, and in the School of International Studies, Jawaharlal Nehru University. She edited *Vanita*, the monthly journal of the Andhra Yuvathi Mandali (1956) and two volumes of *Kavita* (1955). She has translated both into Telugu and from Telugu into English; the latter includes *Modern Telugu Poetry* in English translation (1956). Her stories have appeared in leading Telugu newspapers, in several anthologies over the last four decades and as a collection more recently. Abburi Chaya Devi's story, 'Woodrose,' was first published in *Andhra Jyothi,* Deepavali special number in 1989.

AJITHAN G. KURUP has an M.A. in Linguistics from Deccan College, Pune. He has written and published poetry in English. He was, till recently, Product Manager for a chocolate company in Hyderabad. He is at present a marketing consultant and a freelance writer.

ALLAM RAJAIAH grew up in a peasant family in Karimnagar District, Andhra Pradesh. He writes that his 'school studies were very painful. Each and every upper caste student in the village school tortured [him] in every way.' He went on, however, to obtain a B.Sc. degree from Warangal. He has published nearly 150 stories in various magazines and collections. His work has been translated into Marathi, Hindi and Bengali. He has also written ten novels (of which six have been published), six short plays and numerous articles. He now lives in Adilabad District. Allam Rajaiah's story 'Manishi Lopali Vidwamsam' ('The Desolation Within') appeared in the collection *Bhoomika*. It was first published in *Andhrajyothi Weekly,* 1990; it was also published in Hindi translation in *Hans* in May 1991.

ANAND (P. Sachidanandan) is an engineer by profession. His first novel, *Alkkoottam,* was published in 1970; his second, *Marana Sartifiket* (1974) was translated into English as *The Death Certificate* (1976). He has published another three novels, four collections of stories, a play (1980), and a philosophical study, *Jaivamanushyan* (1991). He is currently resident in Delhi, where he works in the Central Water Commission. Anand's 'Kayasthanmar' was first published in *India Today*, Malayalam edition, April 1990.

ASHOKAMITRAN (J. Thyagarajan) is the author of nine Tamil novels and as many collections of short stories. A good number of these stories have been anthologized in India and abroad, and translated into several languages. He has also written non-fiction on a wide variety of subjects and has edited the Tamil little magazine, *Kannaiyazhi*. His writing is known for its irony and close attention to detail. As a writer he has, in his own words, 'kept away from coteries of literary snobs and elitists.'

K. AYYAPPA PANIKER, a retired Professor of English and Dean of the Faculty of Arts, University of Kerala, is currently Chief Editor, *Medieval Indian Literature*, Sahitya Akademi, Trivandrum. A poet and a critic in Malayalam, he is the recipient of several awards and prizes including the Bharatiya Bhasha Parishad's Bhilwara Award, the Sahitya Akademi Award for poetry, the Kerala Sahitya Akademi Awards for poetry, criticism and essay, the Kuttamath, the Ulloor, the Asan, the Kalyani Krishna Menon Prizes; the Rev. Vadakel Award and the SPCS Award. He has published three collections of poems and two collections of critical essays in Malayalam, and three monographs and three anthologies of literary criticism in English, in addition to editing several volumes of essays.

K. BALAGOPAL is a mathematician by training. He has a doctorate in the subject, and worked as a lecturer in the Department of Mathematics, Kakatiya University, Warangal, from 1981 to 1985. Since then he has been a full-time activist, and is the Secretary of the Andhra Pradesh Civil Liberties Committee. For the last ten years, he has been writing on various issues in both Telugu and English, and is a regular contributor to the Bombay-based journal *Economic and Political Weekly*.

CHAKRAVENU (Chakra Venugopal) held a B.Ed. and an M.A. in Telugu Literature. A research scholar in the Telugu Department of S.V. University, Tirupati, Andhra Pradesh, he was working on his doctorate. He had written eight stories in all when a fatal accident in 1993 cut short a promising literary career. His story, 'Kuwait Savitramma' first appeared in the *Andhra Jyothi Weekly,* July 20, 1990. It also found a place in the Telugu collection *Katha '90* (1992) edited by Vasireddy Naveen and P. Sivasankar.

B. CHANDRIKA, a reader in the Department of English at All Saints' College, Trivandrum, is currently Deputy Editor, *Medieval Indian Literature*, Sahitya Akademi, Trivandrum. A writer of short fiction and critical articles in Malayalam, she is the author of *V.K. Krishna Menon* (1990) and *The Private Garden: A Study of the Family in Post-War British Drama* (1992). She has edited *Best-Loved Stories* (1991) and *Critical Spectrum* (forthcoming).

D. DILIP KUMAR writes in Tamil though his mother tongue is Gujarati. He has published one collection of short stories, *Moongil Kuruththu* (1985); and a critical work on Mowni (1992). His stories have been translated into Bengali, Hindi, Kannada, English and French. He has translated both short stories and poetry from Hindi, Gujarati and English. He lives in Madras, where he is an exporter and library supplier of Tamil books.

MOGALLI GANESH holds an M.A. in Economics from the University of Mysore, from where he also obtained an M.A. in Folklore. He is at present a research scholar in the same university, where he is working on his doctorate in Folklore. His first collection of short stories, *Buguri* (1992), has been warmly received by critics. 'Battha' ('The Paddy Harvest') was published in the collection *Buguri,* 1992.

GITHA HARIHARAN has worked for several years in publishing, first as an editor in a publishing house and subsequently as a freelancer. She is the author of *The Thousand Faces of Night*.which won the 1993 Commonwealth Writers Prize for the best first book. She has also published a collection of short stories entitled *The Art of Dying* .

JAYANT KAIKINI is a bio-chemist currently resident in Bombay. He has published three anthologies of poetry, and an equal number of anthologies of short stories. He won the Karnataka Sahitya Akademi Award thrice; for his poetry in 1974; and for his short stories in 1982 and 1989. 'Dagadu Parabana Ashvamedha' is from the collection of the same title (1989). It was first published in *Karmaveera,* Deepavali issue, 1987.

N. KALYAN RAMAN was educated in Madras and Calcutta. He is a technocrat by profession. In the seventies he published some of his fiction in Tamil little magazines; since then his writing has shifted to reviews and articles on books and films. At present he works with the Indian Space Research Organization lives in Ahmedabad.

SA KANDASAMY is the author of five novels and five collections of short stories. His stories have been included in anthologies compiled by the Sahitya Akademi, the National Book Trust and the Indian Council for Cultural Relations. He has also researched and written scripts, including those for three tele-serials based on novels; these were telecast by Madras Doordarshan. His script for the short film *Kaaval Deivam* won the first prize at the Argino Festival in Nicosia in 1989. He is also one of the founders and the editor of a Tamil little magazine, *Ka Cha Da Tha Pa Ra.* 'Engalloor' ('Our Town'), from the collection *Kandasamy Kadhaigal* (1988), was first published in *Kavanam,* 1985.

KONANGI (Ilango) worked as a Cooperative Bank secretary for ten years in rural Tamil Nadu. He gave up his job in 1988 to devote all his time to literary pursuits. He now lives in Kovilpatti, from where he edits a Tamil literary magazine, *Kalkudharai*. His stories have been published in three collections of short stories in 1987, 1990 and 1992. 'Kopammal' ('The Shadow Game') was first published in Konangi's collection of short stories entitled *Kollanin Aaru Pennmakkal* (1990).

S. KRISHNAN, translator and journalist, has served as Cultural Adviser to the United States Information Service for several years. He is a regular contributor to a number of Indian and foreign journals. A book-reviewer and occasional poet, Krishnan is a senior editor of *Sruti*, the Madras-based magazine of music and dance.

P. LANKESH has published four collections of short stories, two novels, a full-length play and seven one-act plays, and a collection of poems. He has won the Karnataka Sahitya Akademi Award (1987) and the Book of the Year Award (1988), in addition to film awards for direction (1977), screenplay and dialogue (1980). Lankesh has also been a journalist for several years. He writes a column in the Kannada daily *Prajavani* and contributes regularly to English-language newspapers. He is the editor and publisher of the Kannada magazine, *Lankesh Patrike*.. His 'Sahapa-thi' ('The Classmate'), from the collection *Kallu Karaguva Samaya*, was first published in the Deepavali issue of *Lankesh Patrike*, 1988.

MANASY went to school in Thiruvilwamala, a remote village in Kerala. She later worked towards a degree in Chemical Engineering from Trichur Engineering College, but was married before she could complete the course. She has lived in Bombay since 1970, and has recently begun work as a freelance copywriter. Although interested in literature, theatre and music, she would still, 'given a chance, prefer to study science.' Manasy's 'Devi Mahatmyam' ('The Goddesses of Arshabharata') first appeared in *Mathrubhumi Weekly*, March 19, 1978.

THOPIL M. MOHAMED MEERAN lives in Tirunelveli, where he runs a business. He has published two novels and a collection of short stories (1990). His first novel, *Oru Kadalorathu Gramathin Kadhai* (1988), was selected best novel of the year by the Tamil Nadu Kalai Ilakkia Peruman-dram. The novel, a best-seller, has also been prescribed for study in some universities in Tamil Nadu and Kerala. His second novel, *Thuraimukham* (1991) was selected the best novel of the year by Ilakkia Chindanai, and is to be translated by the National Book Trust under its Aadan Pradan programme. Meeran's 'Idhai Eppadi Nirutthuvadhu?' ('How Do We

Stop This?') is from the collection *Anbukku Mudhumai Illai,* 1990. It was first published in *Muslim Murasu* in June 1989.

D.R. NAGARAJ obtained his M.A. and Ph.D. in Kannada from Bangalore University, and has taught in the same university since 1975. Till the mid-eighties, he was an activist in various leftist movements; since then he has 'just speculated on various notions of alternatives in politics and culture.' He has written two books of literary criticism, and writes regularly on social and political issues in *Lankesh Patrike,* a popular Kannada weekly.

E. NAGESWARA RAO was educated in India, the United States and Canada in English/American Literature and Linguistics. He taught for several decades in both North American and Indian universities before retiring as Professor of English from Osmania University, Hyderabad. His books include *Shaw the Novelist (1959), Ernest Hemingway: A Study of His Rhetoric* (1983) and *New Horizons in Teaching English* (1992). He is currently Visiting Professor at the University of Hyderabad.

PADMA RAMACHANDRA SHARMA has translated the works of several leading writers in Kannada, including Poorna Chandra Tejaswi's *Carvalho* and *Men of Mystery,* both published by Penguin India. An English teacher by profession, she has taught in India, Ethiopia, England, Zambia and Malawi.

K. RAGHAVENDRA RAO has a doctorate in Political Economy from Toronto University. He has taught Political Science at Guwahati, Karnataka and Mangalore Universities. He has worked extensively on translation of both poetry and fiction from Kannada into English, including the novels *Parva* and *Vamsavriksha* by Bhyrappa (forthcoming). In addition to his publications on political theory, he has published *The Road Taken,* a collection of his poems in English. He has edited, with P. Lal, *Modern Indo-Anglian Poetry;* and with Kanavi, *Modern Kannada Poetry.* He is currently writing a novel in English.

RAMACHANDRA SHARMA has a doctorate in Psychology from the University of London. He has worked as a secondary school teacher and a psychologist in India, England and Africa. Sharma is considered one of the pioneers of the modern movement in Kannada literature. His publications include *Gestures,* a collection of poems in English. He has translated English poetry into Kannada, and both prose and poetry from Kannada to English. A recipient of the Karnataka Sahitya Akademi Award, his own poems and short stories have been translated into several languages.

C.V. SREERAMAN is a lawyer by profession. His first collection of stories, *Vasthuhara,* won the Sakthi Award and the Kerala Sahitya Akademi Award. Three of the stories in this collection were made into films. One of them was 'Irrikyapindam' ('Obsequies for the Living') which was first published in *Mathrubhoomi Weekly,* June 24, 1973. The story has also been translated into Hindi, Marathi, Oriya, Punjabi and Kannada. The film version, called *Purushartham,* was directed by K.R. Mohanan and the film received national and international acclaim. His novels, Chidambaram and Vasthuhara were made into films by Aravindan. The latter film, Aravindan's last, also won the author the best film-story award.

SWAMY (Bandi Narayanaswamy) teaches in a single-teacher school in a small village in Cuddapah District, Andhra Pradesh. He has written one novel and twenty short stories, and though he is not a prolific writer, his fiction has carved a niche for itself in contemporary Telugu literature. He is also closely associated with the Anantapur Writers' Club, which has been promoting new trends in the Telugu short story. Swamy's 'Vana Rale' ('Rain') appears here. It was first published in the *Andhra Prabha Illustrated Weekly,* March 20, 1991. The story won the first prize in the Ugadi short-story competition held by the *Andhra Prabha* in 1991.

USHA NAMBUDRIPAD holds a doctorate in Linguistics from the University of Kerala. The Kerala Sahitya Akademi published her work *The Social Background of the Address Terms in Malayalam* (1990) based on her

190

research at the International School of Dravidian Linguistics and at the Akademi. She has also translated several books into Malayalam, including four abridged editions of world classics. She is currently working on a project in the Department of Malayalam Lexicon, University of Kerala.

VASANTHA KANNABIRAN is an activist in women's organisations and civil liberties groups in Andhra Pradesh. As part of the organisation Stree Shakti Sanghatan, she has participated in its pioneering research on the role of women in the Telengana Movement. She has contributed to the volumes *We Were Making History: Life Stories of Women in the Telengana People's Struggle* (1989) and *Recasting Women* (1989). She also writes poetry in Telugu. She is currently working with the Deccan Development Society, a non-government organisation based near Hyderabad.

VASANTHA SURYA writes investigative features and articles for major Indian newspapers in English on social issues and education. She has published a book of poetry, *The Stalk of Time* (Cre-A, Madras) and a book of poetry translated from Bundeli Hindi. She also writes in her mother tongue, Tamil.

VAIDEHI (Janaki Srinivasa Murthy) lives in Udupi, Karnataka. She has published four collections of short stories, a prize-winning novel, and a collection of poetry. A collection of her plays for children is in press. She is also a frequent contributor of essays to the Kannada newspaper *Lankesh Patrike*. Vaidehi's stories have been translated into Marathi, Hindi, Tamil, Telugu and Malayalam. 'Summaniralagaddu' ('The Confession') was first published in *Lankesh Patrike*, September 8, 1991.

VIJAYA GHOSE taught at school and college level for several years in different parts of the country before joining the Children's Books Division of Thomson Press as Assistant Editor. Subsequently she was on the staff of the children's magazine *Target* for eleven years. She has been the editor of the *Limca Book of Records* since its inception. A freelance writer and editor, her latest book is *Tirtha, A Treasury of Indian Expressions*.

KETHU VISWANATHA REDDY has been involved in the study and teaching of language in Dr. B. R. Ambedkar Open University, Hyderabad, where he is currently Head of the Department of Telugu Studies. He has also developed teaching material for the South Indian languages for use in the Indira Gandhi Open University. He has been writing short stories since 1960 and has published two collections of stories (1974 and 1991) and two short novels. His short stories have been translated into Hindi, Bengali, Kannada, English and Russian. He has also been editing, over several years, *Kutumba Rao Sahityam*, a multi-volume collection of Kodavatiganti Kutumba Rao's work.

ZACHARIA was born in Urulikunnam, Kottayam District, Kerala. He was educated in Kerala, Mysore and Bangalore. He has taught English in Bangalore and Kanjirapally, Kerala. At present, he works as a consultant for the Malayalam edition of *India Today*; and for the Press Trust of India. He has published five volumes of short stories, a novella and a collection of essays. He won the Kerala Sahitya Akademi Award for his short stories in 1978. Zacharia's 'Theevandikkolla' ('Rajan's Train Robbery') was first published in *Mathrubhoomi Weekly*, October 27-November 2, 1985.

Katha is a registered nonprofit society devoted to creative communication. The main objective of the society is to spread the love of books and the joy of reading amongsts adults and children.